I0650908

WORLD
OF
BONE

WORLD OF BONE

OF

MARSHALL CARROLL

proving
press

Book Design & Production:
Columbus Publishing Lab
www.ColumbusPublishingLab.com

Copyright © 2024 by Marshall Carroll
All rights reserved.

This book, or parts thereof, may not be
reproduced in any form without permission.

Paperback ISBN: 978-1-63337-857-5
Ebook ISBN: 978-1-63337-858-2

Printed in the United States of America
1 3 5 7 9 10 8 6 4 2

1.

ADRENALINE

JANUARY 17, 2033, roughly twenty miles north of the closest town of New Haven, Missouri.

The sky darkened from the overcast of a freezing downpour. It's five till eleven at night. I can feel my hands go numb as the rainfall trickles down from my coat and into my gloves, soaking the polyester. Each warm breath is visible as I exhale into the brisk night air. Looking over I can see Sean's hands trembling as well. He glances over at me, and in what seems to be the softest whisper he can muster, he calls out to me. I don't think I would have even known he said anything if I wasn't staring directly at him.

Sean: "Are we going in, or are we just going to freeze to death?"

I raise my hand steadily, signaling him to hold his composure for a little longer. We need to enter at eleven, the memo had explained with extreme emphasis. Not a minute sooner and not a minute later than eleven exactly. Sean's gaze falls back down to the cold steel of his compact. He checks the safety as he cocks it back another time to triple-check that he had chambered a round.

When he looks back up at me, I can see the faint shimmer in his eyes as the moon briefly peeks out from behind the overcast. He whispers to me yet again.

Sean: "How much longer, Jale?"

I shake my head politely as I peer down to my watch, checking the time again.

"We've still got two more minutes. Be patient, Sean, and keep as quiet as you can."

I follow Sean's habit and check the chamber of my Five-seven, assuring myself once more. This is the worst part of any of these memo tasks. The patience you have to have before anything even happens. The tasks themselves may be hard at first, but after so many years, they get easier. But the tense feeling beforehand never fades. The buildup of pressure, of doubt, it's like the fear of the unknown. But as soon as the clock strikes time, the adrenaline starts pumping throughout your body like a spark that ignites everything. After that, the moments from start to end feel like meager seconds passing by without any thoughts at all. I look down again just as my watch counts down. I raise my hand, counting down from five, to signal Sean in the door. As I reach zero the door handle gets shot off and Sean rushes into the door. Following him into the open corridor that spans wide to the left, we both instinctively form together to clear the room. Sean's raspy voice calls out into the seemingly desolate house.

Sean: "FBI! Come out without a fight and we won't have to hurt you!"

Alice Marie Holand, the target from the memo, a rogue agent

suspected of being sent by either the British SAS or Russian Spetsnaz. Extremely skilled and extremely lethal. Worked with her on several memo tasks, from assassination to counterterrorism. I've seen what she can do with a small blade, let alone a rifle, and to think we are approaching her in her own home. Like moths willingly flying into the spider's web. As we round the corner, we can hear her in the distance shuffling around. Sean looks back, whispering again.

Sean: "Do you think she's scared?"

I shake my head as I snicker from the comment.

"No, she knew we were coming. If anything, she's starting to feel the adrenaline. We should be the ones trembling."

Sean's focus glares down at the door as Alice stops shifting around. She calls out to us.

Alice: "Sean Landon Reyes, how wonderful of you to stop by, and if you're here, that must mean they sent him along as well—am I wrong?"

Sean hesitates, looking over to me. I nod back as I reply.

"Alice, you don't want this fight. It'll just end with one of us dead. You know that, don't you?"

I hear her laughing as she responds.

Alice: "Oh Jale, you don't know the half of it, do you? You're pretty well known even amongst the elite in special forces. So why did you, a man of such great talents, recuse yourself down to the FBI? It's not an agency worth your abilities. Simple arrests and small tasks that anyone with half a brain could carry out."

I signal Sean to follow close down the hall toward the door as I take point. Opening the creaking door, Alice steps back, taking a defensive position.

Alice: "Well it seems you were able to track me quite easily."

I hear a shot fire through the wall as Sean falls down holding his shoulder in pain. I drag him to my side of the door, returning a few shots in the room.

"Come on, Alice, give yourself up and come out!"

She doesn't respond, but I can still hear her in the room. I move Sean into a relaxed position, having him hold pressure on the wound. The bleeding slows to a stop. Sean looks up at me, apologizing for not being able to help.

"Trust me. I'll handle it. Just stay here and continue to hold pressure. It's not a large wound, so just wait for more agents to arrive. They'll be able to get you out. Stay with me, Sean, you hear me?"

Sean: "Y . . . yeah I hear you. I'll be fine. J . . . just go."

Moving down the hall to the second door, as quietly as I can to catch her off guard, I slam it in, firing a few shots before rushing in to knock her off balance. She falls back reaching for her knife as I slam my boot on her hand and keep my gun aimed on her. She winces in pain as I keep myself over her.

"It's over, Alice. Either surrender and come peacefully, or you'll force my hand."

She looks up into my eyes; as I meet her gaze, I feel a deep unease. I said before that patience and waiting were the most difficult parts of these kinds of tasks. The task of assassination—where in the end you and your target come face to face, one way or another—in that moment there is a profound respect, almost an intimate moment in which they know they've been bested. However, Alice doesn't have that look when our eyes meet. She smirks up at me, narrowing her eyes, but doesn't utter a single word. As I'm looking down, I can hear a faint unfamiliar voice. It seems to be directed at me.

Voice: "Jale, look behind you."

I reposition myself with my gun still aiming down as I circle around Alice. I glance upward to see a fully upright Sean walking toward me.

"Sean! You shouldn't be moving. Your shoulder is . . ."

I focus toward his previously injured shoulder, and it's completely fine, even the blood from before seems to have vanished.

"How did you—"

Just as I start to mutter the words, Sean pulls his gun up on me. As I go to aim back, Alice kicks toward me, sweeping my feet from underneath me. I try to regain my composure, but she wrestles my gun from my hand.

"What are you doing? Sean, shoot her!"

Sean holsters his pistol as Alice kicks away from me and rises to her feet. Sean speaks up as she pulls me to my feet.

Sean: "Sorry, Jale, this is how it has to be."

Gritting my teeth, I glare over at him. What reason could he have to forsake not only me, but all of our countrymen? For this traitor? For some kind of compensation? None of it makes sense. I need answers.

"Both of you are betraying your own country? Who are you both working for? What country put you up to this? Answer me!"

Alice starts to laugh as she reloads another magazine into my gun, pressing it to the back of my head. She's mocking me, dancing around the truth. The very same people I had trusted to watch my back are now driving a knife into it. That condescending tone of hers. I wish I hadn't hesitated before. Damn it!

"What's so funny?"

Alice: "Only you proving my point when I said you don't even know the half of it. We aren't betraying our country, your country is betraying you."

"What!?"

Alice: "Still not catching on? With every administration, one thing remains the same no matter who it is. They need someone taken out of the picture for good. This time it just so happens to be you. You joined the FBI after retiring from the special forces so suddenly, it sounds like someone feared you getting closer to the executives at the top. That's why they commissioned me as well as Sean here to prevent that from happening. A little precautionary measure for one of the best that special forces had to offer."

As I stare down at the worn wooden floorboards, I sigh in disbelief.

"Well? What are you waiting for?"

I hear the gun cock back and then a loud shock wave bursting my ears. An immense pain rushes through my body, and it feels as if it freezes over in seconds. Then suddenly nothing. I can't even feel the floor beneath my feet. As instantaneously as a flash of lightning, the cold feeling fades. The same voice from before reaches my ears, this time like it is right in front of me.

Voice: "Jale . . . Jale . . . Raise your eyes and look."

Slowly I manage to return to consciousness. I can see an older man sitting across from me. A doctor? I regain a feeling across my body—this time it's warm, like the heat radiating off a fire. My lips feel dry and chapped, and my eyes feel bloodshot as I try to hold them open and focus.

"W . . . where am I? Who are . . . you?"

Old man: "Jale, relax your body. Only move when you're ready to."

I start to drift between a dreamlike feeling and a state of consciousness. I can't tell how long I am awake or even if I am awake at all. I lie still for a while to build my strength up before I can push off the ground at last. An old man still sits across from me. His face looks soft, and his company feels almost comforting.

"Are you . . . a doctor?"

The old man lets out a hardy laugh. Looking around, I don't see anything other than him in the room. The walls and even the floor are a bright white, almost blinding from the light gleaming overhead.

Old man: "No, I'm no doctor at all. From the looks of it, though, you figured that much already."

"So who are you?"

The old man looks over at the rustic oak door before he starts again.

Old man: "I am no one in particular, just an old man helping a poor soul that came to me."

"I appreciate it, but I still don't know where I am. I need to get back—"

The old man stops me mid-sentence.

Old man: "I'm sorry, Jale, but . . . there is no going back now."

"What? What do you mean? Where have you taken me? How do you even know my name?"

The atmosphere in the room changes. It's no longer comforting as we both sit in silence for what seems like hours. After that tense moment of extended silence, I calm myself and take a few deep breaths.

"I'm sorry for my tone."

The old man merely shakes his head at me.

Old man: "No, no, be at ease. It's not an uncommon reaction for those who have come here."

"But where is here?"

Old man: "Why, the afterlife of course!"

2.
CONSCIOUSNESS

I LOOK PAST THE OLD MAN in disbelief, and see him noticing the paleness coming over me.

"After . . . life? Does that mean you're . . . God?"

The old man scoffs in a humorous manner as his eyes shift down and his body relaxes.

Old man: "No, no, nothing like that. I am not here to judge you. I am merely here to send you onto the next realm of existence. In simpler terms, I will reincarnate you."

I hesitate for a while trying to come to terms with it all. Am I really dead? What happens now? What about the life I had lived before?

Old man: "Calm yourself. You can take your time moving onto the next world. Ask me those questions after you can breathe more than one syllable at a time."

The old man lets out another hearty laugh as I start to lie back and slow my breathing.

"Sorry for thinking out loud."

Old man: "Oh, no, you weren't. I could see it in your face and eyes. After you've done this for as long as I have, you get acclimated to the expressions and emotions of others. I can practically hear what someone is thinking when they openly display such strong feelings."

"You can . . . hear my emotions?"

Old man: "My friend, there's quite a bit of what you would call miracles that I can perform. It comes from both the understanding through experience as well as a collective consciousness. They work in conjunction with one another."

"Collective consciousness? What do you mean by that?"

Old man: "You called me God earlier, right? Well, that's not exactly incorrect, but at the same time, completely incorrect. We all are God in extremely small ways."

"Wh . . . Sorry, I think you are losing me here."

Old man: "Hmmm, let me see . . . You know of Adam and Eve of Christianity, don't you?"

"Of course, the progenitors of humanity itself."

Old man: "They were given consciousness by God. They were given God's consciousness split between the two of them. Then they bore children, and God's consciousness was split even further. Over time God's consciousness divided itself between all living things, be it humanity, or the wildlife around us, or the nature that is carried through the vegetation. All of it contains a small piece of God, and that is a collective consciousness."

"But then doesn't everyone have the same amount of consciousness, if it's divided constantly?"

Old man: "It varies per bloodline. The more a specific bloodline creates descendants, the more the consciousness will divide. I, for example, am of the one thousand thirty-ninth bloodline in human history. That is when I put an end to my bloodline through my faith in the church of Christ. Little did I know that because of this, my mortal soul would transcend to a higher plane of existence. Hence why I stand before you with greater power than that of many of humankind."

"What about me then? What is the strength of my consciousness, sir?"

Old man: "Galahad, call me Galahad, my friend. As for your question . . . It is hard to say without a demonstration of power. Your experience in combat and conditioning of your body over the course of your life should grant you a bit of control. But control alone would be like . . . It would be like trying to ignite wood without a flame."

"So does all of this mean that Christianity is the true religion? You made the comparison earlier to Adam and Eve."

Galahad: "Oh, no, no, don't get caught up in those details, Jale. In fact, I still do not know exactly what religion this consciousness stems from. Never mind that, though, let us see to testing your ability."

"How will we do that?"

He stands up, his frail body steadily making it to the wall. I watch, confused, as he places his hand against the pale structure. The room starts to shift, and the wall shatters from the ground up. My eyes widen in amazement as the room we had been in was broken into small shards. Outside the room is an expanse of grasslands that stretches for miles, with rolling hills in the distance and a stream that is so clear you can see all the way to the bottom.

"That's . . . impossible . . ."

Galahad smirks and raises his hand into the air, closing his eyes while doing so. As he folds his hand into a fist, the shards from the room start to rise and encompass us. They form back together like the pieces of a puzzle, and before long, the bright room from before is reconstructed around us.

Galahad: "Your turn."

"What?! I can't do that. I don't even know what that was, let alone be able to recreate it!"

Galahad: "You don't have to recreate it."

"Huh?!"

Galahad: "I had no bearing on what just formed. Everything you saw—the way the room opened and the view beyond—is inherent in me. In my case the shattering of the room like glass shows that this frail old man, as you think, can overcome purified diamond walls with ease."

"Purified diamond?"

Galahad: "Indeed the strongest material within earth's domain, which I reside over."

"What about the grasslands? What do they represent?"

Galahad: "Ha, ha, now you are catching on. The biome itself will represent the elemental nature of your consciousness. In my case, grasslands represent the nature of earth. Maybe it has something to do with ruling over it as my domain. Not even I fully understand that yet."

"Amazing, simply amazing."

Galahad: "I've told you everything to the point of my understanding. Now it is time for you to gather your understanding directly from experience. Hold your hand up to the wall and try to channel your consciousness into it."

"But how?"

Galahad: "No! No more questions on the matter. Experience it yourself! That is how you must overcome."

I place my hand against the wall as he instructed; it's completely smooth. No way to even grip it to crush it like glass. If I lean my weight into it, my hand slides up, slipping right off. I push my hand up against it, trying to get it to do anything at all. My eyes are closed as I focus everything on channeling my consciousness. I'm not even sure what that means, though. Logically it's not fathomable, yet I've seen it with my own eyes. Is there a trick? A button? Maybe even a hologram? No, nothing of the sort.

"I don't understand. How can it even be possible? It's not logical at all!"

Galahad: "You're overthinking it, Jale. If you try to use logic, you'll only strain yourself unnecessarily. You are completely correct, logic deems that certain, but we aren't using logic in channeling consciousness. I know it sounds ridiculous to do it without thinking, but trust in me."

"I do trust you!"

Galahad: "Then stop thinking in terms of what is possible and impossible. I did not use any special method or deception; it is only channeling, nothing more and nothing less."

I reposition myself and this time place both hands on the wall. I clear my mind of everything and just focus on the feeling of my hands against the wall. Again nothing. I lower my head and my mind starts to flood with memories of my life, or to be more accurate, my past life. I remember home, the dry desert air in the summer. The memory of the coarse sand feels almost overwhelming. Before I know it, I feel the vibrations radiating from the surface of the wall.

"How is it . . ."

Galahad places his hand on my shoulder. I quickly look over, but he shakes his head, calmly pointing to the wall.

Galahad: "Keep focusing."

Turning my concentration back to the wall, I find that it keeps trembling before settling once more. I step back, looking over to Galahad, still slightly confused.

"I couldn't break through."

Galahad: "No, you couldn't, but we have seen where you are and what you need to build upon. To be able to make it rumble like you did takes great control; you're only lacking in power. If you have this much control right after learning about consciousness, imagine what you could do in a year, what you could do in a decade. Follow my guidance, and you will be able to overcome any hardships that may come."

"But where do I go from here? You said the bloodline itself controls the consciousness and therefore the amount of power. Doesn't that mean it can't be enhanced further?"

Galahad: "Don't you remember what you are here for in the first place?"

I sit deep in thought for a few minutes as Galahad patiently awaits my answer.

"Wait—the reincarnation!"

Galahad can't help but smile and nod his head.

Galahad: "Precisely, my friend."

3.
BLOODLESS

GALAHAD STEPS BACK from me and rests himself on an old wooden chair. As he shifts his weight, the chair settles underneath him. He seems to relax before he addresses me again.

Galahad: "The time is drawing near for your reincarnation. I need to explain only a little more. Please hold your questions, so I can get everything out."

"Understood. By all means, continue."

Galahad: "Reincarnation was probably a bad way to put this. It's more like resurrection. You will still have memories from your past life; try not to reveal any of this to others. You're likely to experience more of a struggle in the next life if you let it be known that you've been resurrected. Upon revival, you will immediately feel considerably stronger from gaining the second consciousness. Be aware, however, this doesn't mean you will be impervious to harm. There are others who know of this power and will do anything to steal it from you."

Galahad stops, looking straight into my eyes.

Galahad: "Those who may commit such atrocities, they need to be struck down. Waste no pity on those who would slay the innocent and make the world into a living hell just to become stronger. In return, Jale, you will grow stronger and stronger as my apostle. Once you attain a stronger consciousness, you can return here of your own volition."

"What about my previous life?"

Galahad: "I'm sorry, you will not be able to return there. If you're asking about the ones who betrayed you, then worry not. They will get what comes to them. If that doesn't satisfy your anger, then you should aim it at me."

"What? Why would I be angry with you?"

Galahad: "Had I not spoken with you during the last moments of your life, you wouldn't have hesitated to take the lives of both of them. We wouldn't be having this very conversation. I'm sorry, Jale."

My fists clench in frustration as he explains what he did.

"Just like that, everything I once had is gone. You took that away from me. Anyone would be furious. Frustrated at the very least. It isn't something I'm going to forget anytime soon. To know I could have gotten out of that alive, yet you intervened. Who wouldn't be upset with you?"

Galahad: "Jale, I—"

"I'm not finished. I won't forget it anytime soon. However, I can't just sit and dwell on it at the same time. I've been fighting all my life. It would have caught up with me sooner or later. I am angry with you, Galahad, but I'm angry at myself, as well, for not being strong enough to handle it despite your intervention. Nothing I can do about it now anyway. Just drop it; I don't feel like staying on this topic any longer."

Galahad: "Thank you, Jale. I believe you will become greater than even I can become. Maybe you'll even be the savior of this world going toward its ruin."

I let out a sigh as I ponder the thought. A savior? No, I'll never be that.

My body grows heavy. My hands suddenly feel numb, and as I look down to them, they fade away like a mist. Before I can mutter a word, my body jolts up in another unfamiliar place. Light shines through on the other side of a tattered curtain. As I gaze around the dimly lit room, I try to make out as much as I can. I'm in a makeshift bed, where I can feel coarse sand as I shift my body. The walls are cracked and decrepit; they look almost claylike. As I unwrap a cloth draped around me, where my body had once been, there is now merely a skeleton.

"Wh . . . what?"

I bring my hands up to my eyes, and they're all bone. In a panic I jump to my feet and look around the room. I stop as I look over to a shattered mirror in a nearby room.

"No, it can't be . . ."

I lean against the wall and try to contemplate what's happened.

"No, no, no, this has to be a nightmare. What even am I?"

I slam my fist against the clay wall, and to my surprise it completely collapses to the ground, and on the other side is a vast expanse of sand. The wind blows a little into the decrepit clay structure.

I fall back from shock and lie there in complete disarray. My body—or to be more accurate, my skeleton—feels immensely strong, but . . . I'm at a complete loss for thoughts, let alone words. Folding my head into my hands, I try to calm down.

"I need . . ."

I stop as I take in a deep breath. I can feel myself taking in air like normal, but my chest doesn't expand. Reaching through my bones I can go all the way through my ribs to the back without feeling anything in between.

"How is this possible? I'm not dreaming, I feel completely awake."

I collect myself and stand up, once again looking into the shattered mirror.

"I can see without eyes, breathe without lungs, and even move with no muscle or joint tissue whatsoever."

I sit down leaning against the wall, as I let my mind wander. Does it even matter what I may look like? What if others are out there like me? Maybe this entire world is filled with different forms completely foreign to me. I need to be prepared to face anything regardless of what appearance it may have. Besides, I can't do anything about it regardless of how I feel.

Breathing a sigh of relief as I finally have calmed down from my episode, I move each of my joints slowly. Come to think of it, what do I even call my own hands? Even my head really isn't one, just a skull. I breathe another sigh as I ponder the question. For the sake of simplicity, I will still refer to my body as if it is normal. If I get caught up in those small details, I won't make much progress figuring out where I am.

"Well, if I have no choice, I need to get acclimated to this form. It doesn't seem any different apart from appearance, anyway."

As I start to calm a bit, I notice my surroundings, and see that Galahad is absent. A small hole in the wall demands my attention. I check constantly, making sure no one is listening in or trying to come in. The wind's whistling would easily cover up someone's approach. I just really hope this little shanty doesn't belong to anyone.

"The sun sets to the west and the moon's to my right, so that must mean left is west. Well, even if that's not exactly right—things could work differently in this world—I'll go with that for now. That being said, where should I go?"

I think about it before deciding to head to the west, where the sun had set. It gives me the most nighttime as possible. That way I can hide my appearance better and not be out in the heat of the blazing sun. Cloaking myself in cloth, I head out into the sands.

I can feel the smooth sand beneath my feet; it shifts between the bones and feels weird with each step. I need to get some form of sandals or boots to trek across this barren landscape. It's just sand for miles, not even any sign of vegetation, no cacti or even any change in the sands. Normally, you can find at least small changes in the desert ground. That also means a greater likelihood of civilization.

"I just hope I can find something. Even a small settlement would do. Or even a small trail would give me some sign of life."

As I cross the last dune, the ground levels out like a sandy pasture. The flattened land widens my field of view. I'll gladly take this over climbing all those dunes.

"Hopefully this means I can—"

As soon as I start, I hear a step behind me and then a voice. It's a higher pitched voice, which almost sounds like that of a young girl.

Young girl: "Show me your hands and turn, slowly!"

I turn slowly as I raise my hands up from the cloth. I see her mouth agape in fear.

Young girl: "You're, buh . . ."

"Buh?"

Young girl: "Bloodless!"

4.
SCRAPPED

SHE POINTS a peculiar-looking gun at me that's almost like a flintlock but the barrel is a bright bronze. I can see the grip peeking out from her hands. It has a pale white color, reminiscent of ivory. The girl's face is partly covered by a mask, and her hands and face have flesh, unlike mine. I take advantage of her hesitation as I bend her wrist inward, loosening her grip before I knock the gun down and pull her into me. She loses balance, and as she falls back, I hold her in place. Her face goes from startled to terrified as she starts to panic.

Young girl: "No! No! Stop, get away from me! I don't want to die!"

"Calm down!"

She starts struggling and flailing her arms wildly. She pushes away from me and falls, and the back of her head smacks against a stone half buried in the sand. Moving her off the rock, I check the back of her head. To my shock, she isn't bleeding, but that blow she took made her pass out.

"Hey, are you alright? Can you hear me?"

Sure enough, she is unresponsive. I hold her wrist, and I can feel her pulse. It's elevated from her struggling, but that's to be expected. I'm just relieved to feel one at all after her fall. I keep trying to get her to wake up but to no avail. After a short while, I curiously pick up the gun to look it over.

"The barrel is in a hexagonal shape. Back home this would have been an antique. All the metal looks nearly brand new, though. This world must not be as advanced. I need to know if there is any rifling."

I point the gun down into the sand and fire. The gun goes off and the sand disperses all around us. Just in case, I pull the trigger again, but nothing happens the second time. The gun opens from the breech as I go to inspect it.

"It's a smoothbore, single shot, breech load, made from bronze and with a hexagonal barrel. This world might predate even the Civil War."

I look over toward the girl who is still unconscious even after I fired the gun. Figured that might have woken her but it hadn't. Walking over to her, I reach down to her mask. I remember this from somewhere; it's a plague doctor mask. She couldn't be a doctor, though, considering how young she appears. Taking her mask off, I'm appalled by what's underneath. Where her eyes had been are now merely the sockets. No skin like the rest of her body, only the bone outline.

"Wha . . . what! Her eyes are like . . . like mine."

Putting her mask back on, I let out a deep sigh. Who could have done something like this to a girl this young? Now I understand why she had the mask on. Trying not to think about it, I shift my focus down to the holster she has on. Strapping the gun in place, I take it off her and tighten it around my chest. Picking her up, I hoist her onto my back and adjust the cloth around my body. For a few miles I retrace my steps back to the clay shack before she wakes up again.

Young girl: "Wh . . . where am I?"

"Not sure, I was hoping you could tell me."

Young girl: "Where are you taking us?"

"There's a small little shack around here. You can rest for a little while before I start questioning you."

Young girl: "I don't have anything to tell you. Just let me go."

"You hit your head pretty hard back there. Are you sure you'd even be able to move well enough on your own?"

The girl doesn't say a word. I start trying to get her to open up.

"Do you have a name? I'll give mine first. It's Jale."

We finally get to the little shack, and I set her down before I sink down against the wall.

"This sand is so rough on my feet."

She looks over toward her gun and holster that I had taken.

"You aren't getting this back, you know."

No response again.

"Well?"

Young girl: "W . . . well, what?"

"I asked for your name. Mind giving it?"

Young girl: "It . . . it's Fayne."

"Alright, Fayne. How old are you?"

Fayne: "I'm twelve."

Fayne brings her knees into her chest as she plays around with the sand on the floor. Picking it up and watching it fall between her fingers.

Fayne: "Why did you bring me here?"

"I already told you. You hit your head pretty badly back there. I wanted to make sure you had some shelter from the sand where you can rest up enough to be able to move again. How are you feeling?"

Fayne: "Lightheaded, hard to focus."

"Think it'd be a good idea to be trekking anywhere like that?"

She faces away from me, looking out the doorway.

Fayne: "You mean you're not going to scrap me?"

"Scrap you? What do you mean?"

Fayne: "You mean you really don't know?"

She lifts the mask from her face, revealing her eye sockets that I had seen before.

Fayne: "They take as much of what they can use as possible from any living creature. I got lucky for only losing my eyes. I was given this mask not long after, and it helps me sense what's around me."

"What?! How?!"

Fayne cowers back from the tone of my voice, and she starts to speak nervously.

Fayne: "I . . . I'm sorry . . . I don't know!"

"Oh sorry, I didn't mean to sound so aggressive. Back to the main point: Who are they?"

Fayne: "They're called a lot of things, but mostly they're called scrappers because of the way they use people's bodies like materials. Everything from the bones and flesh, even the blood."

I gasp in disgust and horror. It's downright sickening what these people are doing. Using people like animals that are going to the slaughterhouse.

"I think that's enough about that. I'm gonna be sick if we continue."

Fayne: "How are you Bloodless then?"

"Huh?"

Fayne: "It's said the Bloodless are scrapped down to the bone, but you didn't even know what scrapping was."

"Maybe I lost my memory of it. I don't know."

I obviously lied to her, but I also don't want her questioning me further on it.

"Let's talk about something else. Where are you from? Do you have a home? Are there any places nearby that we can go to?"

Fayne: "Yeah. There is a place in the northwest."

"We will head there in the morning. For now, get some rest."

Fayne: "Wait—where are you from?"

I can't just tell her the truth. Even if I did, she might not believe me anyway.

"Don't you think it's rude to ask where someone is from when you haven't answered that very question?"

Fayne: "S . . . sorry."

I lean back against the wall as Fayne starts to fall asleep.

At daybreak, the sun shines brightly throughout the shack. Fayne is still asleep. I wonder why she didn't try to run off in the middle of the night. Does she really not know where we are either?

"Fayne . . . Fayne, the sun's up and you should be as well."

She rubs her eye sockets as she stumbles to pull herself up.

"Fayne, which way is the nearest town?"

Fayne: "T-town? You mean the districts?"

"Is it somewhere we can find a place to stay, a job to earn my keep?"

Fayne: "They have all sorts of vendors, but I don't know about an inn. I've only been there once before. It's about an hour walk to the northwest."

I want to go at night, but with the girl as she is, we need to get there as soon as possible. I might not feel hunger any longer, but I can't say the same for her.

"C'mon, we have to get going so we can get there and still have time to look around. Are you okay to be moving now?"

Fayne: "Yeah but, wh . . . why are you looking after me like this?"

"Huh?"

She looks up at me with blood-like tears running down her face. It's terrifying and heartbreaking at the same time. It must be like that because she lost her eyes. I didn't think she was able to cry at all.

Fayne: "I tried to hurt you yesterday. So, why . . . why are you being so kind?"

I wipe the tears from her face and pick her up onto my back as we start to head out.

"I guess I just couldn't bring myself to leave you behind on your own."

Fayne: "I was going to scrap your body to keep on living."

This sends a disturbed chill down my spine, but as insane as it is, I can't help but to keep her with me. It's hard not to feel pity for her.

"I've been in the face of danger more times than I can count. I don't hold it against you. However, if you'd be so kind to guide our way as an apology, I wouldn't stop you of course."

She giggles slightly and holds onto my back tighter and responds gleefully. For having as cruel of a time as she has had already, it's relieving to see the childish innocence still shining through.

"Thank you, Jale."

I let out a small laugh that stems from her cute burst of joy as we continue toward the district.

5.
QUARRY

I FINALLY CAN SEE the first glimpse of what I presume to be the district. As we draw closer, I can barely make out the gate at the center and the wall that expands out from each side of it. As the wind bellows, the gate can be heard rattling its hinges, trying to swing open against the locking mechanism. It's almost as if the wind is beckoning us in. Sand is built up on the sides of both gate doors, swept up from when the gate has been opened, leveling the ground out in front of it.

"Fayne, this is it, right?"

Fayne: "Yeah, this is it. It's one of few places that people can feel safe while staying in the confines of the walls."

I make it about a hundred feet from the decrepit gate before stopping. The wind now settles as I gaze over the top at the guards on the garrison. They begin to open the gate, and I can hear their voices yelling at one another but can't quite piece together what they are saying.

"Fayne, will they let me in?"

Fayne: "Keep your hood up. Just because this is a safe haven doesn't mean people are very social."

"You okay to walk on your own now?"

Fayne: "Yeah, my head feels clear now."

I set Fayne down. As she trots slowly through the gate, I follow behind, nervously mumbling to myself.

"Here at last."

I half expect the lookouts to stop us because we appear suspicious, but nothing. No one reaches out, no voice yelling out to us, just like it's normal. Looking around I can see others sitting on the sides of the roads. Looks like a refugee camp from the middle east in my old life. There's a dreary atmosphere about it. I can feel the sense of anguish looming over. With clothes that look more akin to rags, some of the squatters are bandaged up as if they were caught in some kind of skirmish recently. The best dressed ones look straight out of a history book with cotton tunics or robes, headdresses not unlike what I've seen from Arabic communities. Streets are all coarse sand that packs beneath you as you step. Way easier on the feet than when I was sinking down every time I took a step out in the desert. After walking for that long, it felt as though I would pull my leg up from the sand without my foot. Like losing a shoe after getting it stuck in the mud. Livestock are corralled beside the small shanties that make up most of the living space. The stench reminds me of fairgrounds back home. As Fayne and I move deeper into the district, the buildings grow taller and the stench from before fades. Fayne turns back to me as we stop to look around.

"Are you hungry?"

Her stomach growls, and she blushes before nodding her head. I chuckle and look for anything resembling a restaurant. Even a butcher or tavern would work. In the distance I see the start of stalls with quite a few people heading that way as well.

"Think we can find something to eat this way?"

Fayne: "Yeah!"

She seems gleeful as she grabs my open hand. I start leading the way, but suddenly I can feel Fayne yanked away from me. I jerk my head around and come face-to-face with a plump, burly man holding a knife up to Fayne's throat. A raggedy beard lines his menacing smirk, and just to the right of it, a scar runs down his jaw and onto his throat. He has a firm grip on the blade as I see his muscles tense up from behind his sleeve.

"What do you think you're—"

Suddenly a gun cocks behind my head.

"Ah, I see now."

Burly man: "From your reaction, this isn't your first time in this situation, huh, stranger? You know how this works, don't you?"

He lets out a heavy laugh. I hear a raspy snicker from behind me.

"Yeah, you could say that I know exactly how this will end."

Burly man: "C'mon then, what are you waiting for. Hand everything over, or we'll just have to take the girl instead."

Fayne panics and struggles against the man, but he tightens his grip and covers her mouth. Letting out a slight laugh, I pull my hood back and both are just as terrified as Fayne had been when I met her. As I have my hands raised beside my head after pulling my hood back, I slam my elbow into the gunman's hand behind me, throwing off his aim from my head. Turning to face him, I grasp the pistol by the barrel while my arm wraps around the bend in his elbow, forcing it straight into an arm lock. He pulls his arm back in a panic as I push the gun against his hip before bringing it up his side and jamming the barrel into his ribcage. He stumbles back in pain as I create distance between us while shifting my aim to the burly one who is still armed.

"This ends with both of you left bleeding in the sand."

Stepping away from the one on the ground, I strafe to the right giving me space between them. The burly one still has Fayne. These problems were always a stalemate experience in my past life, hard to handle due to the unpredictable nature of your enemy. Even if I manage to take them both out, if Fayne is hurt in the process, I won't consider it a success. It's not a favorable position to be in when there is only one of me and two of them. A third person steps out from the alley. Whoever they are, they seem to be approaching cautiously as if they know what's going on. Another of these degenerates?

Burly man: "What is a Bloodless like you doing in this district?"

I keep his focus on me and the gun still trained on him. His partner gets back to his feet. He's a smaller, scrawny guy, the burly man's complete opposite in physical appearance. I retort the question by trying to pry more information out of him and keep both distracted.

"What do you mean? I go where I please. Nothing more and nothing less."

The scrawny one tries to slowly creep forward toward me, but before he can take a single step, the burly man lets go of Fayne. Shocked, the scrawny guy turns to catch Fayne, but she slams her shoulder into him and runs my way.

Fayne: "Jale!"

She quickly spins behind me. The burly one who had been holding her hits the sand completely limp. The suspicious figure stands behind him with a bloodied knife. The scrawny one panics, lunging toward them. I take the shot and his body crashes down to the ground.

"Who are you?"

Stepping out into the light, it's a woman with short crimson hair who is wearing a loosely wrapped amber-colored tunic. It's sleeveless and stretches down to her knees forming a skirt-like trim. Her skin has a glistening tan, slightly darker than her clothes.

Mysterious woman: "I could ask the same of you. Those men were my quarry, and I don't intend to share."

"What do you mean?"

She gives me a puzzled look.

Mysterious woman: "Didn't know that people still weren't aware of the presence of bounty hunters. These two were wanted across four districts for several heinous crimes. Laws are nonexistent, so us bounty hunters have lots of work coming in. In a sense I guess that would make us the law."

Mysterious woman: "Reina's my name, and you are?"

"I'm Jale. This is Fayne."

Fayne is still hiding behind me.

Reina: "So, what's a Bloodless like you doing in one of the districts?"

"I guess my main priority now is to get a lay of the land. I'm new around here, so all this is an experience to say the least."

Reina: "And the girl? Is she your slave?"

"What!? Absolutely not."

Reina sheaths her knife and lets out a sigh of relief.

Reina: "As I said before, there's no law anywhere around. Theft, murder, arson, and yes, even slavery isn't out of the question with anyone. These two were some of the most renowned slavers, hence why their bounty was quite an undertaking."

As she finishes, we can both hear Fayne's stomach churn from hunger. Reina smiles as I turn my attention to her again.

Reina: "Tell you what: help me take these two back, and I'll treat you both. After all, I only did half of this job, and I dislike the idea of letting a favor go unreturned."

"Alright, lead on then."

She manages to get the scrawny one over her shoulder, leaving me to carry the burly man. My initial reaction upon lifting was to put full force into it. Not realizing my strength yet again, I manage to not only throw him over my shoulder, but above my head to the other side. At the sight of this, Reina smirks and gives me a wise remark.

Reina: "Easy, killer. They're already dead."

Shaking my head, I once again hoist the burly man over my shoulder. This time securing him.

"Alright, where to?"

Reina: "First, pull your hood over. Not many people would be welcoming at the sight of a Bloodless."

I do so, and she begins walking from the alleyway. Following close with Fayne, we make our way toward a different section of the district.

Reina: "This building here, it's the bounty office as well as the local tavern. Top floors are reserved for meetings, negotiations, and collections of bounties."

The building has three stories that rise above the other structures in the district thus far. From the shanty houses to the mossy brick storefronts, it stands over all of them.

Reina: "Leave our two bounties out here against the wall. They'll be out to check them in a short while. Afterward, you can take anything off them you need besides their clothes. Maybe after the bounty collection, we can talk a little more business if you're interested, Jale."

"I'll think about it. C'mon, Fayne, you're probably starving at this point."

We sit at a small corner table in the tavern, and I order the lunch special for Fayne. Reina gives the waitress a few copper coins, then excuses herself to the top floor.

6.
OFFERING

FOR A WHILE we wait in silence. Fayne finishes her meal as I rest the side of my head on my hand. Reina is taking her sweet time as I grow impatient.

"Fayne, stay right here. I'm going to check what's taking so long."

She nods at me before I turn and make my way up the steps. Before I make it to the last step, I can already hear Reina's muffled voice and another from behind the first door.

Reina: "Come off it. It's ridiculous to ask this of someone who just arrived. Besides, we don't even know if he will help us at all, let alone asking him to do something so dangerous so soon!"

I make out what seems to be a man's voice responding to her.

Man's voice: "From what you said, he seems like he can handle himself. Taking out one of those criminals was already a tremendous help. Reina, trust my judgment. He could be a great asset to us."

Reina: "I could have handled both those lowlifes myself, and you know that. Besides, you're also asking me to take a pay cut in order to split the rewards with him. I still need to eat, y'know?"

Man's voice: "Reina, I'm aware of your capabilities, and yes, you could have. But that isn't the point here. It's not a matter of doubting your skill but rather inquiring about his."

Reina lets out a sigh. I can barely hear them.

Reina: "This was my quest. I took this on my own, to finish on my own."

Man's voice: "What is wrong with having a little help? Reina, just follow my request and guide him for a bit."

Reina: "And what of the girl? She still isn't in any condition to be moving freely and would slow us down, putting all of us at risk."

Man's voice: "She can stay within the guild chambers. We still have room."

Reina: "Fine, do whatever you want. Just know that I still have the right to complain about it."

The man lets out a laugh, and I hear Reina walking toward the door. As she opens it, she looks at me in surprise but shrugs it off, closing the door behind her.

Reina: "C'mon, we will get you settled in the chambers first before discussing anything."

"Lead on."

She takes me back downstairs to Fayne, who is passed out on the table. Reina smiles as she picks her up and carries her to a side door of the tavern. It slides open, revealing a somewhat desolate hallway with several doors on the left side.

Reina: "These are the guild chambers. Yours is the fifth door here on the bottom floor."

We walk into the room, which only has a single candle on a nightstand between two beds. Reina lays Fayne in one and sits on the edge of the bed. She invites me closer and hands me a small box.

Reina: "I don't know how much you heard of my conversation with the guildmaster, but I'll sum it up. The coin is for helping me take in those two from earlier. Their belongings were transferred to me, but the gun was confiscated by the guild. I am also to confiscate your gun. Guild policy is to do so for any shooting incident that occurs in the district. That being said, witnessing it myself, I know you weren't in the wrong. So I added in the coin they had on them as a trade for it. Simply place your gun in the box and take out the coin pouch inside, and that matter will be settled."

I open the small box, and the coin pouch lies there open with twenty-some tarnished coins that look like pennies. I scoop the loose ones back into the pouch and tie it off, taking it out of the box while placing the gun I had gotten from Fayne into the box.

"Thanks for this, Reina. So what's next?"

Reina: "That depends on whether you take me up on my offer— well, more like the guildmaster's offer."

"And if I refuse?"

Reina: "You'll only be able to stay here for a week, at most. After, they will either kick you out or offer you the room for a price, including back pay for the week you already stayed. Which normally ends in people being kicked out, because ten copper coins per week is rare outside completing quarries."

"Not exactly a comfortable position you've put me in."

Reina: "Now don't go blaming me. It's the guildmaster who wanted to enlist you as a bounty hunter in the first place. No offense, but while the guildmaster may trust you, I still err on the side of caution."

"No offense taken. In fact, that's a very levelheaded way of thinking. What would I be helping you with?"

Reina pauses with a sigh as she glances over at Fayne, who is in a deep sleep.

Reina: "The guildmaster wants me to take you along with me to an encampment west of the district."

"Why?"

Reina: "Those two from earlier were criminals from that encampment—only petty ones but still dangerous. Took us months to track them down just to find out they were working right under our noses in our own district. There is no way those two idiots could be mindful enough to be that discreet."

"So someone's masterminding their movements? Keeping them under the radar?"

Reina: "Radar? What?"

"Oh sorry, I meant they are being told how to keep their business out of sight."

Reina: "Right, and this area is where we believe their stronghold is. Jale, this won't be an easy task. We are to investigate the area, and if we find the head of this nest of criminals, we will put an end to him ourselves."

"I don't suppose you have a plan then?"

Reina: "Unfortunately, not really. There is a ridge hanging over the encampment that would give us a good vantage point. Scouting it out would be easy from there. But what we do after we find our target—I'm at a loss."

"Nothing we can really do about it until we see it for ourselves. Then maybe we can come up with something. No use worrying. Let's get some rest and talk more about it in the morning."

Reina: "Alright, tomorrow we have to get up early anyway to head into town and get you suited up."

"Huh? What do you mean by that?"

Reina: "You'll see in the morning. 'Night."

With that she walks out the door, closing it behind her. I look over at the other bed where Fayne is sleeping. She probably just had one of the longest days of her life. I don't blame her for being drained. Speaking of which, I'm not doing much better. Guess I'll rest my eyes till morning. No good if I can't stay awake come tomorrow.

7.
LUCID

I CAN HEAR A VOICE calling out to me in the distance. Is it morning already? Reina must be coming to get me.

Faint voice: "Jale, can you hear me?"

Wait, that isn't Reina or Fayne. I pull my hand to my face as I'm blinded by a bright light.

Faint voice: "Welcome back, friend."

As the light clears up, I see Galahad standing in front of me in the same room we were in before.

"Galahad?!"

Galahad: "I have to admit, even I did not expect to see you back here so soon."

"Likewise. Last time I was here I had died. Is that the case this time as well?"

Galahad: "Oh, no, that is not the reason. You have become lucid in your unconscious state. However, having just attained this state, I imagine we don't have much time, so make your questions light."

"How did this happen? Is this like a dream?"

Galahad: "It seems I can communicate with you this way because you have absorbed another's consciousness and rendered yourself lucid in the process. I'm not sure if this can quite be called a dream though."

"I absorbed someone else's consciousness?"

Galahad: "It certainly seems that way. If that is the case, you will be able to search their memories."

"What? How would I be able to—"

Galahad: "Jale, you mustn't keep asking yourself *how* before you have even tried. Now search back into your mind and reveal the way."

I concentrate on trying to recall the memories of the other consciousness. But how do you remember something you never experienced? I'm not even sure whose consciousness I absorbed. I retrace my steps in my mind, from when I first got here, back to the flattened sands where I met Fayne, to the hike across the desert. Then back to when we first entered the district when those two men had grabbed Fayne.

Galahad: "What do you see?"

"Something is different; it's as if I can see it from their perspective."

Galahad: "That must be the other consciousness."

I focus on them, and I can see myself from behind, being held at gunpoint. But where do I go from here?

Galahad: "Try and remember what they looked like, the way they spoke, anything about them that might trigger a different memory."

As I focus on them, it's as if my own memories start to fade and I become them. I look down at my hands—they're flesh and blood now.

"What the hell is going on?!"

Then I feel someone grip my shoulders, and as I look up, the burly man stands before me.

Burly man: "Hey, pay attention. We have a meeting with the boss before we go back to the district."

My body feels as though it's moving on its own as I follow him into a courtyard surrounded by open desert with a few cliffsides casting a shadow over me. As I look around, I can make out seven houses in an L shape, with the largest one in the corner. The burly man leads me into it, and as the door opens it reveals a large tavern with a balcony above and the tables all full. Some of the people look like simple merchants, while other soldiers and cutthroat lowlifes are drinking themselves stupid.

Burly man: "Almost there now. This is your first time seeing the boss, isn't it?"

We go behind the bar and out a small gate. It leads back outside where a tall man has his back to us, presumably their so-called boss.

Boss: "You will not fail me again, understand?"

My body jolts back up as I gasp heavily for air, as if I had just reached the surface of water after holding my breath.

Fayne: "What's wrong?!"

I hold my head in my boney hands.

"What the hell was that!"

Fayne: "It . . . it was a nightmare, wasn't it? I get those a lot, too, when I'm anxious."

I calm my breathing as I glance over at Fayne, who is behind Reina.

Reina: "Are you alright? The way you were shaking, it seemed like you had a meeting with death himself."

Rolling over to the opposite side of the bed, I pick myself up and lean against the wall, still in a bit of shock.

"Sorry to have worried you. Just give me a minute."

Reina: "Take your time, but don't stall too much. We still have a few stops to make."

That dream felt so surreal, seeing everything so vividly. Was I really seeing another's life through their memories? Divinations, lucid dreaming, even being resurrected in the first place—it's all so overwhelming. What is the overall purpose Galahad has sent me here for? In the beginning, he told me I was to be his apostle, as if I would even know what that would entail. At what point will all this come to a head? Guess the only thing I can do is keep moving forward; it's the only way I will find out for certain. Recollecting myself, I make my way back out the door, and Reina gives me a nod as I follow close behind her.

"Where exactly are we headed, Reina?"

Reina: "Well, you can't exactly be wearing tattered rags forever, can you?"

"Yeah, that wouldn't look great on my part, to keep the same clothes, I guess."

Heading out the front of the tavern and into the main sandy path, Reina turns toward the marketplace. Originally, we were headed there yesterday but were stopped just short. Reina turns toward me and Fayne, who is slightly in front of me.

Reina: "Don't worry, I don't think anyone is bold enough to try something on us now. Even with that in mind, still watch out for pickpockets—won't matter how much of a threat we are if we are robbed blind before we even realize it."

The market stretches for what seems like miles, each vendor set up with simple table stalls, all with the same spacing. Occasionally between the stalls are stairs leading up to larger indoor stores.

Reina: "It's a good place to stock up, but also a great place to be swindled. My advice? Stick with the indoor stores for general goods like clothing, food, medicine, and things like that. But anything of a miscellaneous nature is where you'll have to risk the outdoor vendors."

"I assume you didn't bring us here without something in mind?"

She smiles and signals us to follow behind her. She starts heading down a side alley and into a store tucked away on a side road off the main drag.

Reina: "Right this way."

We follow her into the shop and are immediately surrounded by all sorts of hides and tanned leather hanging from the ceiling.

Reina: "He is a bit eccentric but a fine craftsman. Lanson! C'mon, don't be a stranger. You have customers!"

Lanson: "Hold your temper, Reina. Imma comin'!"

A scrawny man slowly struts out, a cane in his left arm supporting him. His leg looks awfully sore, and his back is hunched.

Reina: "Good to see you're still as mobile as ever."

Lanson ignores her as he grumbles something inaudible to himself and hobbles toward me.

Lanson: "I can already guess you want me to fit this big oaf of a man, right Reina? First time I would be fitting a Bloodless though. Discretion would be preferable, would it not?"

"How did you—"

Lanson: "The way you carried yourself down the alley, your footprints left a pure skeletal print a normal foot could never make. I'm a tailor, boy. I have fit countless people over the years. Give me more credit. If anyone should notice an abnormality in someone's movements, it should be me!"

I look to the side as Lanson lectures me on his own ability. Seeing what Reina had said about his eccentric nature, I just sit and listen. Before I know it, he starts taking measurements around my torso.

"Hey, what are you doing?"

Lanson: "Stay still! This will take too long if you don't, and I want you out of my store as soon as possible!"

He takes no time jotting every measurement down and scurrying about his shop, tossing pieces of equipment this way and that. Reina holds back laughter.

"For a guy with a bad leg he sure can get around."

He unwraps the cloth I was using to cover myself with, revealing my full skeletal form. After which he throws a loose tunic toward me. With its darkened coyote-brown color, the garment looks worn down from prior use, but it's still fully intact. I slide it on and put the greaves on too.

Lanson: "Now you're looking a bit more equipped and way better than in those rags from before."

"Thanks for your help, but how much is it?"

Lanson: "We aren't done here yet, you fool. Here, these go on next, over the tunic."

Reina smirks. I'll bet she is enjoying having someone else be on the receiving end of this bickering. The next piece is a leather cuirass that you could tell was no stranger to abuse. It fits over the tunic almost like a plate carrier would. However, in place of Velcro are two straps woven together on either side. They connect both to the backplate and the bracers that fully cover my boney arms.

"Is that all?"

Lanson: "What, you wanted more?"

"No, no this is fine."

Lanson: "Then be gone with the both of you!"

"But what about—"

The man hobbles away and slams a door in the back before I can even ask him how much he wanted in return. Reina walks us out the door.

Reina: "That crazy loon owed me a few favors. I assume this was his way of repaying me for them. Don't sweat it, he has never been one to pinch at someone's purse."

"Seems like he more than makes up for it with his charm."

Reina cackles as we continue back to the bustling market. We step onto the street as she pulls boots from her satchel, a pair for each of us.

Reina: "I also snagged a few pairs on my way out, because I knew he would forget them."

"You stole them?"

Reina: "And you are my accomplice. Now hurry up and get them on—both of you."

She makes it sound so normal. I take the larger boots from her hands, then she turns to help Fayne with hers. I slide mine on and strap them across, then I pull the loose hood of my new tunic over my head as we get back out in the marketplace.

Reina: "Next and last, you will need more firepower for this job. If you let me take all the credit and money for this bounty, consider this a gift from me."

"No issue for me to do it that way."

Reina leads us deeper in the bazaar to several stands lined with everything from fine scimitar-like blades to shoddy makeshift rifles. She picks up a decent-looking rifle and tosses it over to me before slamming a coin purse on the stand.

Reina: "Twenty-nine copper. Take it or leave it!"

The stand owner smirks and swipes up the bag, handing it off to someone beside him as he hovers his hand over a holstered pistol. I instinctively tense as the other man counts out the copper, and I feel like my nonexistent heart is going to burst. The man looks back over and nods as he takes his hand away from his hip, and I follow suit. I breathe a sigh of relief as we walk away with the long rifle in hand and Reina leading on.

"What the hell was that, Reina?!"

Reina: "Can't handle a little tension?"

"That was too sudden for you not to have clued me in beforehand. What if I reacted more aggressively?"

Reina: "Who knows. Life would be boring if your heart didn't race from time to time. Rather die excited than live depressed."

She snickers as we make our way back to the hall.

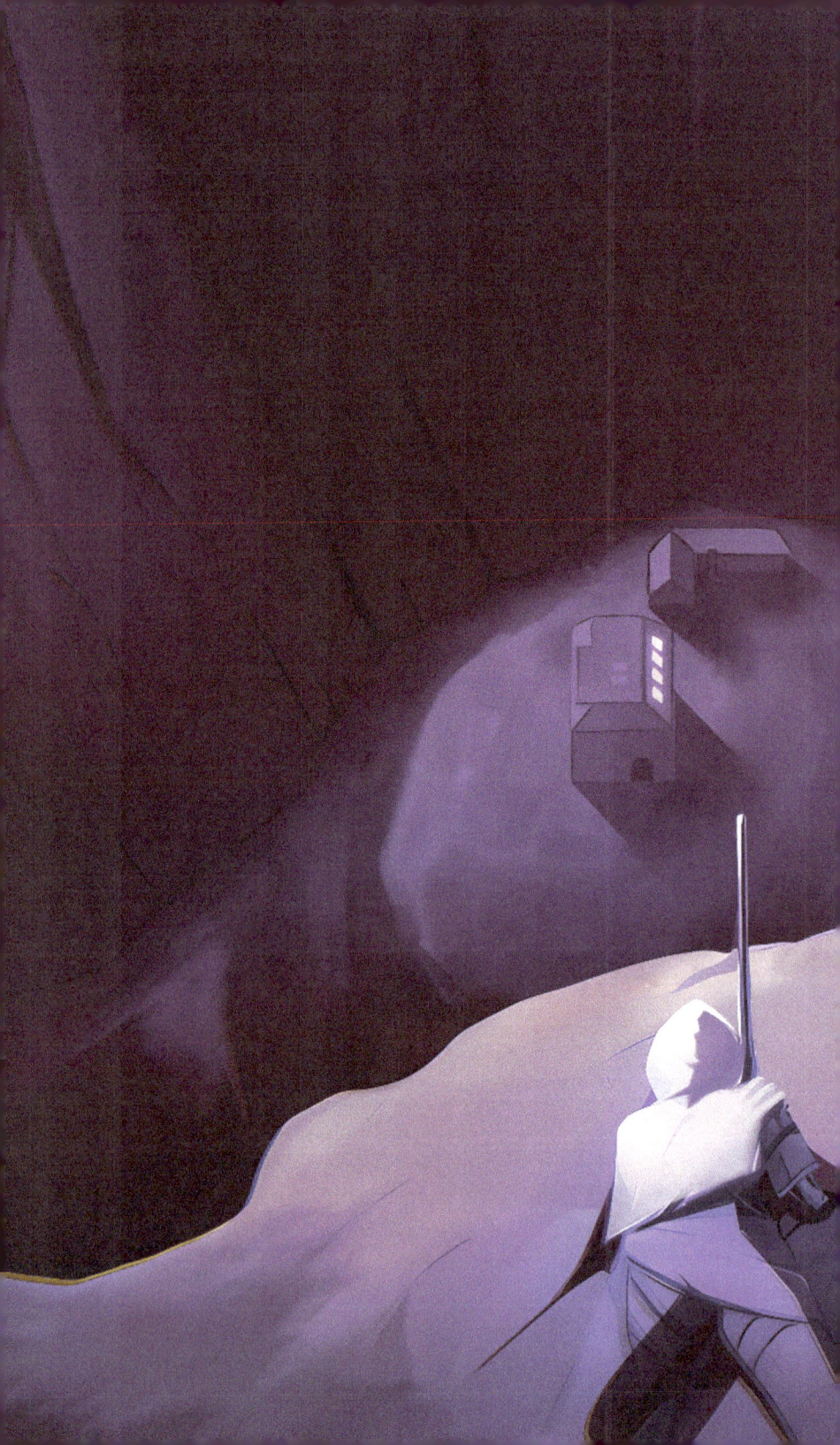

8.
UNSETTLING

WE ARRIVE BACK AT OUR ROOM as Fayne stumbles inside in front of me. Before I can follow her in, Reina pulls me back.

Reina: "Hold up, Jale. Come with me to my room for a sec."

"What's wrong, Reina?"

Reina: "We need to plan out what we are going to do tomorrow."

"Tomorrow is when we are setting out? Kind of a late heads-up, don't you think?"

Reina: "No time like the present, right?"

"Fayne, I'll be back."

She nods back at me before lying back in her bed. I close the door and make my way up the stairs, sticking close to Reina.

Reina: "I'm going to need to take that rifle back now."

"Of course. You bought it after all."

We get to the upper floor of the rooms. As she opens the door, I see the massive collection of maps arranged upon the wall. A few rough-looking tables are gathered in the same corner of the room as the maps. Tools stand lined up in slots on the backside of a workbench beside the tables.

Reina: "Here, hand me that rifle. I think you'll appreciate this."

I toss it to her, and she snags it out of the air and lays it down on her workbench. She begins tinkering and pulls several tools up from their slots. I can just barely make out a cylindrical piece she has in front of her. After she brushes a darkened polish over the stock, the whole rifle has a new black stain that cradles the silvered barrel. A brand-new scope sits just above and in front of the breech.

"Talented one, aren't you?"

Reina: "I'm a jack-of-all-trades, really. Even apprenticed with Lanson for quite a while before the guild office opened up."

"And where did you get this?"

Reina: "Oh, the scope? Let's leave questions you don't want the answer to unanswered."

I let out a small sigh before brushing her comment off.

Reina: "Alright. So with what I told you yesterday, you know there is an overhang above the encampment. Here, you can see it on this map."

She leans over the table and pokes a small nail in the center of the map, then puts another pin with red dye next to the first.

Reina: "And this is where the encampment itself is."

"If they are smart, they'd understand anyone looking for them would use it to get the drop on them."

Reina: "Be ready to face some small resistance along the ridge. Oh, and here, I almost forgot."

She fastens a few pouches to my new tunic on the left and right sides.

Reina: "You know how this rifle works, right? Just a breech load. First, rotate this piece here to access the chamber. After that, take the cartridge here and slide it in. Close the breech, pull back the hammer, and you're ready to fire."

"Right, thanks for the heads up."

I already figured that out, but it's nice to see how much she knows, plus she might assume that my knowledge is suspicious considering I only had a pistol on me before.

Reina: "Wanna set out now?"

I take in her smirk as she leans back in her chair.

"Moving out now, you wouldn't have to worry about the heat. Not only that, but the lower visibility would give us an edge in taking them by surprise. As you said before, no time like the present, right?"

Reina leans back up and pulls a satchel off the back of the chair as she uncovers a small sheath, looking back up at me whilst looping the sheath through her belt and tossing the satchel on the other side.

Reina: "I figured you would say that."

I nod toward her as she loads up a map as well as a few odds and ends from the corner table. Getting a better look at the sheath, I see that it's a khukuri, and just as she turns back I catch a glimpse of a holster on her opposite side.

"Ready now?"

Reina: "I have spare cartridges for that rifle of yours in the satchel and of course a few extra for my pistol as well, besides what is in the pouches."

"You already had the cartridges made up?"

Reina: "Truth is I didn't just pick that rifle out at random. I've been eyeing it for quite some time. Come on, we will be back before Fayne even realizes we left."

I head out through the door as she locks it behind us, and we creep down the stairs. After reaching the front door of the dimly lit guild lobby, I let Reina pass me as she guides us out into the desolate streets of the district.

"You're the one with the map, so lead on."

Reina: "We will head out the west side gate. I don't have a mount, so we are hoofing it across the sands."

"Can't be helped. With these boots, though, the ground shouldn't put as much stress on my feet."

Reina: "You call those feet?"

I can't hold back my amusement as we pass through the gate.

"Already comfortable enough to be taking jabs at me, huh?"

Reina sticks her tongue out at me as I cough out a laugh.

"You're a child."

Reina: "And what exactly do you mean by that?"

I think about it for a bit as we cross over the seemingly endless dunes. The waning moon hangs over us with a faint red tint.

"Free-spirited would be a better word for it."

Reina: "Are you making fun of me as well, Jale?"

"Only a little, but don't change that about yourself."

Reina: "If I knew you better, I would say you were worried about me."

"I don't know if worried is the proper term for it. With everything I have seen, I know that a gloomy place like this can get the best of anyone. It makes me hopeful to see you can still laugh amongst all of that."

Reina: "Of course, if I wasn't able to stay positive and laugh, even in the face of hardships, well, I think I would have been either dead or Unsettled by now."

"Unsettled?"

Reina: "Yeah, just like those who are lost, still wandering in the badlands. Sometimes they not only lose their minds; their physical forms change as well."

"Just keeps sounding better by the second, doesn't it?"

Reina stops, grinning back at me as she stretches her arms up.

Reina: "Welcome to paradise, Jale. How long will you be staying?"

"I have a special reservation for despair."

Reina shakes her head as her grin grows to a smile.

Reina: "Seems you haven't lost the comedic touch either, Jale. Tell you what, if you keep up your spirits, then I will keep up my own."

"Sounds like a fair deal to me, Reina."

Reina: "Shouldn't be a whole lot farther now, maybe a few more strides ahead. We will try to get there before the moon is soaring directly above us."

The start of the canyon ridge comes into view. Looking at the shifting sand, it appears someone was here, and recently.

"Reina, the tracks are pretty fresh."

Reina: "Yeah, we need to keep our guard up as we continue on. No point in turning back now. Come on."

Reina draws her pistol as we push up to the flat part of the ridge. I can see the encampment far off in the distance, even from the vantage point of the ridge. We stop to survey it as the moon starts to shine at our backs. I lay prone on the cool sands as I prop the rifle up and peek into the scope. I have maybe four-times magnification through the lens at best. Out of my peripheral view, I can see Reina watching my back, scanning the surrounding area.

"Clearly not your first time doing this. Prior bounties, I assume."

Reina: "What are you seeing, Jale?"

Even with the scope, making out the shapes of people isn't easy. Rather than making out exact people, I peer across the landscape for movement, spotting six figures shuffling through.

"Maybe six or so people who are out right now. What are you thinking?"

Reina: "Just keep looking. I'm going to take a look around here."

"Be careful, Reina."

The soft crackling of the sand beneath her feet gets quieter as she moves off in the distance. Returning my eye to the scope, I focus back on the figures. Four of them are gathered around a central building, while the other two are on opposite rooftops. We expected them to have some people up here on the ridge, but nothing so far. Backing off the lens, I listen in to my surroundings and glare across both my left, where the path back down the canyon is, and to the right, where I can hear Reina shifting about in the distance. Keeping myself low, I call out to her.

"Reina, seeing anything over there?"

She doesn't respond right away, so I cautiously pick up the rifle and make my way behind a sizable boulder. From here I can hear what I assume is her from beyond the other side of the rock, so I call out yet again.

"Reina, are you there?"

This time she responds.

Reina: "Jale, you might want to see this."

Stepping out from behind my cover, I lower the rifle and look up to see Reina hovering over several mangled bodies. The lacerations indicate that they were mauled by a bear. Surrounding us are makeshift tents. Counting them up, there's five total. Each one of them seems to be able to hold three to four people comfortably.

"What happened here? Did you see anything, Reina?"

Reina: "No, they were already like this when I got over here. Let's check all the tents and make sure no one is left. It's possible, but somehow I doubt it."

"Let's get to it."

9.
PARADIGM

THE MOONLIGHT AIDS ME as I lift the first tent curtain and peer into it, rifle facing forward out of caution. Two more bodies and too much blood. I nearly miss the cots under them blending in with the damp crimson floor.

"Reina, anyone still breathing over there?"

Reina: "No one was in this tent. It looks like a storage tent."

"Anything useful?"

Reina: "If you clear the rest of them without me, I will sort through everything in here."

"Leave it to me."

I move to the other tent beside me before checking the one beside the storage tent. One seemed like a food-prep area, and the other was empty with the exception of a few more cots. Finally coming back out to the center and creeping up to the central tent, I am stopped by Reina emerging back into the center.

Reina: "Alright, I still have a bit left to dig through in there, but let me take a look at this one with you."

"What are you looking for among this wreckage?"

Reina: "Anything useful really, but what I would like to find most of all are any documents that might clue us in to the operations of the main encampment. This is an officer's tent from the looks of it, so any documentation is most likely in here."

I lift the veil of the largest tent as she follows close behind. It seems like a commanding tent, with a table at the center and several papers either ripped up or stained with blood from a nearby corpse. The corpse is wearing rather more formal attire than the other dead, and seemingly was clutching onto these papers at the time of his demise.

"What do you make of this, Reina?"

Reina: "Sorry, Jale, I have to ask something rude of you, but can you step out of the room while I get all the papers?"

"I get it, you still can't trust me entirely, huh? No hard feelings. It isn't anything I'm not already used to."

Turning to step outside, a question stirs in my mind.

"Reina, how is it you trust me with a rifle on the journey here but not with the documents in this tent?"

Pushing the tent flap out of the way, I step outside and prop up the flap with my rifle, all whilst scanning the cliff edge as she explains.

Reina: "We had quite a long trek here in the open desert. If you wanted me dead, you had ample opportunity to do so without anyone being the wiser."

She shuffles through all the parchment.

Reina: "Meaning either you have no intention whatsoever of harming me, or you are lying in wait until I discover something that would require you to take drastic action. Letting you confirm that I have received specific intelligence would be unwise."

"Very true. I respect your decision, but for what it is worth, it's the former."

Reina: "You are hard to read, Jale. Your trust in me is unprecedented. You turn your back to me and give me ample opportunity to strike at you while your guard is down."

"Do it if you plan to. No sense keeping me waiting."

Laughing through my words, I lean more into the rifle.

Reina: "You laugh in the face of death. Is it fun?"

I shrug my shoulders as I hear her approaching from behind. I assume she has settled everything she needs to. Then I feel her press a finger up against my spine.

Reina: "Bang! Got ya, Jale."

She starts chuckling abruptly as I shake my head.

"What am I going to do with you, Reina?"

Reina: "Hell if I know, Jale. We can talk more later, though. I still need to go through one last box in storage before we head to—"

Mid-sentence she pauses as gunshots and an explosion ring out like a roar of thunder from a wild storm in the distance. Reina takes off running back toward where we had been watching the encampment.

Reina: "Shit! Jale, move!"

I take off after her and hit the ground beside her as she pulls out a telescope, and I peer through the rifle's scope.

Reina: "Can't see anything with all the canyon dust being kicked up. That blast from earlier—could it have been a landslide?"

We wait, just observing, as the dust settles back to the ground after what feels like forever. Trotting away from the encampment is a lone rider, one hand hanging onto the reins as the other droops down at his side, casually making his way out of the canyon as if nothing had fazed him. His horse is as pale as my bones, and as he trails closer below us, the rough-looking saddle becomes more apparent. I focus back on the now-toppled central building; the adjacent buildings don't look much better.

Reina: "After he leaves the canyon, we need to see what the hell happened in there."

As the rider gallops out of sight, we turn back the way we came, up the overhanging cliffside, and descend to the sands below. I hadn't noticed it too much before, but now hiking back down, the ground turns from solid dirt and rock back to the shifting sands of the desert. We are nearly at the base of the ridge before a voice calls out to us, and Reina stops dead in her tracks. The rider upon his pale horse appears, waiting on us as if he had known we were there all along. His darkened skin looks baked in the sun, his face scarred and battle-worn. A slight patch of freshly trimmed facial hair seems to be regrowing as it clings to his chin. This man has the presence of a commander, looking down upon us even after dismounting his horse. Using a stern but natural voice, he captivates our attention.

Rider: "You two, I am certain I hadn't left anyone alive up that way. Tell me, who are you?"

Reina draws her pistol and steps back, while I hold the rifle down but ready to shoulder, if need be.

Rider: "I asked you a question. I wouldn't test my patience if I were you. Your answer could even save your lives."

He glances over at me as I begin to speak, pushing his long jet-black hair from his face. It reveals the gleaming red irises of his eyes—a chilling stare even in the heat of the desert.

"But that also means our answer can put our lives at risk?"

Rider: "You are more intelligent than I give you credit for, Bloodless one. Fine, I'll give you the courtesy of my name first, then tell me yours."

Reina: "Fair enough."

The rider turns back to his horse as he grapples its ebony saddle, pulling himself up effortlessly. It just dawned on me that he hadn't wavered a moment at the sight of my Bloodless form.

Rider: "My name is Solomon, the Grand Sin of Wrath. Your turn."

Reina hesitates, and I can see her slightly tremble as she struggles to speak.

Reina: "My companion and I are bounty hunters. This is Jale, and I go by Reina."

Solomon: "Bounty hunters? I see, then we have no interest in each other. Seems your quarry is likely dead already. Slaughtered due to my handiwork. I suppose there's no point in concealing my reasoning. I need to purge those who stand in the way of my conquest. Greed is in the way of that, and if you are to ever ally yourselves with him, you can count your blessings before I put you under."

"Conquest? What is the meaning of senseless slaughter? You said you gave reasoning, but I don't see it like that. Seems you are no different than this Greed you despise."

Reina: "Jale, shut it!"

She gives me a stern look as we both back away more before Solomon roars back.

Solomon: "Do not compare me to Greed! He wishes to toil in the shadows and control people like puppets! There is no meaning in that life, in my eyes. You cannot live with strings pulling you into the despair of his districts. In this vast desert, the only way to feel truly alive is in the midst of battle. To put your own life in jeopardy and to fight for what you believe in. I do not wish to control anyone, rather wishing this place to return to the true badlands, where the strong thrive. That is life's paradigm. The weak do not deserve to live in misery, to become enslaved by either a master or by despair itself. Jale, Reina, you both have the heart of warriors who can stand and fight. I admire that about you. Maybe you do not agree with my vision, but know that it is not based in senseless bloodshed. It is to free this world from control. Enough of my speech, it will only push my temper that much more. May we cross paths again."

With that he whips the reins. As his pale horse speeds off, we lose sight of him in the vast sands. Reina slowly falls back into the sand, breathing a sigh of relief.

Reina: "The Grand Sin of Wrath, a warrior without equal, stood with us face-to-face after single-handedly wiping out that encampment. Then you retorted him without so much as a change in your voice. You are either extremely brave or stupid."

She snickers as she pushes herself back up, splashing water from her canteen onto her face to refocus herself.

"You alright? Didn't mean to give you any worries."

Reina: "Well you didn't exactly do a good job of that. Pissing off a Grand Sin is akin to suicide for mere bounty hunters like us. They are basically warlords with massive political influence, controllers of resources, commanders of vast armies, all with their own motivations to occupy this land. Thankfully we made it through unscathed. That could have ended in disaster, you know? It is what it is, though. Let's move on to see if we can recover the bounty."

"Roger that."

Reina: "You know you say the strangest things sometimes?"

I shake it off as we head to the main gate of the slaver outpost.

10.

CONDEMNED

SMALL PIECES OF GRAVEL trickle down the walls of the canyon every now and then, reminding us of the looming threat of a shift in the structure. Dust in the air is so thick, it's as if sandpaper was grinding my bones. Wooden support beams lining the path creak as we continue down it. Almost as if they're cackling at us as we pass by.

"We need to hurry it along, not getting a real cozy feeling in this valley."

Reina: "Can't argue with you there. Damn dust isn't comfortable to breathe in either."

She starts coughing into her arm while walking; I can't help but notice my lack of doing so. Maybe it's this body—guess without any lungs or throat, you wouldn't really be able to cough in the first place. But at the same time, how can I feel myself breathing at all? Not that it even matters at this point.

"Reina, how exactly did you plan on doing this in the first place? It's rather convenient that Solomon came when he did. To be quite honest, he saved us the trouble of doing this ourselves."

Reina: "Guess you have a point, but I planned on collapsing the canyon with explosives to topple this place from the start. No way we could have started a gunfight with them and expected to come out alive. Wrath saved me a hell of a lot of resources by doing it himself. In the end, as long as we return with proof of the bandit leader's death, we are set, regardless of how it was done."

"Think there are any survivors?"

Reina draws her pistol once more, spinning it casually up to a low ready position.

Reina: "Won't matter if there are. We need the body whether we get shot at or not. If we come under fire, we simply shoot back."

We pass by what used to be the entry gate; both watchtowers to the sides of the gate are in ruins. The gate is in shambles, caved in by the rubble. Reina slips through a narrow gap, and I just barely manage to push through it to the other side.

"It's a shame it would have collapsed one way or another. Whether by Solomon or by us, this canyon would have met the same fate."

Reina takes a more rigid tone with me.

Reina: "These people are the lowest of the low, nothing but slavers making money from suffering. A shame? They get no such sympathy from me. They can rot for all I care, Jale."

"Reina, think about what you said."

Reina: "Why the hell should I?"

"They're slavers. Who else do you think is here besides them?"

She stays quiet for a moment as she looks down at the ground.

Reina: "You're right, Jale, I have thought about that quite a lot. I don't disagree with what Wrath said though; these people have been condemned to this without reason. They suffer because they could not resist the cruelty of these people. Even if the cold hard truth is that they died in the collapse, isn't that a form of salvation from their pain?"

"Maybe so, but if I had even the slightest chance of saving them, I would seek that path out first before any other."

Reina looks back up, rubbing her eyes. I place my hand on her shoulder.

"It's alright, Reina. Just remember, the road to hell is paved with good intentions."

Reina laughs as she straightens her posture. We continue throughout the base.

Reina: "I really don't know what to make of you, you know that, Jale?"

"How so?"

Reina: "Such a threatening outward appearance, yet you have a calming nature about you. The strength of a brute, yet your thinking is so philosophical. Many people in the badlands are illiterate and rely on their strength to move forward. The few that are intelligent often lack strength. Even fewer are those who have both yet have not a single ounce of compassion. It's inspiring to see someone compassionate enough to lend a helping hand, intelligent enough to know how, and strong enough to do so."

"Means a lot, Reina, thanks."

Never thought of myself as compassionate before. Being trained from the age of eighteen as a soldier. Following orders without question. Taking others' lives simply as a means to an end. Look where it got me: plunged into another chaotic desert. Conflict seems to follow me wherever I end up, or maybe I am the arbiter of it. Either way, it's far from what I would consider compassion.

Reina: "Sorry to cut this short, but we really should get our bounty and get back."

Out of all the buildings that were here prior to the attack, only two remain standing. The others all lay in piles of rubble. The splintered materials surrounding them don't resemble any kind of lumber from back home. This world couldn't be any stranger than it already is: The weapons seem antique, yet the cartridges are all modern. Buildings are constructed of random materials. Some are like clay shacks, and some appear to be wood, but but unlike any kind of wood I've ever seen. Powerful individuals, referred to as the Seven Sins, vying for control of the land. All these differences, and yet it will all play out the same. Blood will be spilled simply for the sake of attaining power.

I follow her to one of the remaining buildings, and we can hear the shuffling of people inside—muffled voices and the clanking of something metal. Maybe shackles? Makes sense for the kind of work these sick and twisted people were carrying out here. Whispering over to Reina, I begin to ask her how she wants to handle it.

"What's your plan? Are we going to check inside? Or do you wanna circle back to the main building?"

Reina: "Let's go in. You still have your rifle ready, don't you?"

"Of course."

I push open the door, which leads into a long hallway. Cells line both sides, and the putrid scent of the room hits me.

"What in god's name is that!"

Reina: "Nothing to do with god, I can assure you that. Eyes up, Jale, we have company."

I peer back up after gagging through the foul stench of the rotting blood that is lined up in the center of the room. Slaves that were being held here seem to have broken out of the cages. They now face us down. Several have makeshift weapons aiming at us as they slide cautiously closer.

"Easy, there. We aren't your enemy."

A mountain of a man within the group comes forward, out in front of the rest like a lion protecting its cubs.

Mountain of a man: "We won't surrender our weapons."

"Wasn't asking you to. You got a name, stranger?"

Mountain of a man: "My name is Halister. Most of the ones around me just call me Hal, though."

He pauses for a moment, looking back at the rest as he motions for them to lower their weapons. He turns his view to the door leading outside.

Halister: "And those who kept us as slaves called me number twenty-three. The nerve of these animals. I only regret not tearing their heads from their bodies myself. It turns out you already beat me to the punch with that one."

Reina: "No, not us. A man named Solomon was here before we arrived. Other than you and the rest of your people, me and Jale here haven't seen anyone else. They may have been buried under the rubble."

Halister: "Then what are you here for?"

"The head of whoever locked you here in the first place."

Halister starts moving toward the door. I stand aside as he pushes out the door and into the dawn light. Shielding his eyes from the rising sun, he breathes in deeply. As he exhales, a sigh of relief passes his lips.

Halister: "You help me get my people out of here, and I will dig his body back from hell itself if I have to."

"Consider it done. Reina, you alright with that as well?"

Reina: "No complaints from me."

"Let's get those shackles off all of you. Won't be easy to make a trip back with your hands bound. Think there's a key around here somewhere, Reina?"

Reina: "Looks like if there is, it would unlock all of them. They all look the same. Besides, to make all of them different would rack up quite an expensive bill. Metal craft isn't cheap, you know?"

Halister: "Honestly, it may be with the same man you're looking for anyway. We should check out that building over there, Jale. It seems the rest won't be anything but a waste to search through, considering the state they are in."

"With any luck, you will be right. Reina, can you head back up to the overlook and see what's in that remaining box? Might prove useful, and as you said before, not like anyone here will miss it."

Reina: "I was planning on it, anyway. Might as well take the rest of them with me, and we will meet you back at the base of that overpass. Trade me the rifle. If you run into any trouble, I could support you from a distance."

"Great thinking—here."

I toss her the rifle. She snags it out of the air before handing me her breechloader.

"Thanks for that."

Reina: "Are you forgetting something?"

"What's that?"

Reina: "Can't very well fire either of these without the proper cartridges. Give me your pouches."

I lower my head, glad to have avoided that situation but embarrassed for not realizing it sooner. We exchange belts. Hers barely fits me, and I tighten it all the way down to keep it from slipping off. She loosens mine and wears it diagonally across her chest. Halister looks over his shoulder at both of us as Reina snickers.

Reina: "I think that diet is working well for you, Jale."

Halister: "You two are quite the characters."

Reina sarcastically scoffs back at him.

Reina: "You're a part of our ragtag band of people now—don't go mocking yourself now."

Halister: "We are all condemned now, whether you like it or not."

"Condemned? What do you mean by that?"

Halister: "Greed won't take kindly to you helping us, if word gets back to him."

"Let's just hope no one is left alive to report to him then."

Halister: "All we really can do."

"Besides, wouldn't he go after Solomon before us?"

Halister: "I wouldn't bet on that. If Greed is smart, he would know that only a Grand Sin such as himself would be a match against another Grand Sin. No, Greed won't risk his pawns in a battle he knows they won't win. As for us, on the other hand, as Reina put it, we are just a ragtag band of people."

"A surefire, safe target."

Halister: "Weird way to phrase it, but I think I understand, Jale. Yes, that is why we are condemned to being hunted down like animals."

What does Greed seek to gain by enslaving these people? What of Solomon? As powerful as he may be, he still risks himself in this kind of confrontation. What is his intent? What could motivate or force him into taking matters into his own hands like this? All this destruction by a single person; what if an army was alongside him? Beyond that, it could draw in other Grand Sins, as well. Forget the destruction of a canyon. At that point, a desert-wide catastrophe wouldn't be out of the question. Great, yet another brewing war, and I've been thrust right into the center of it.

11.
REAPER

SIDESTEPPING HALISTER and emerging from the building, we start making tracks past all the debris to the central building. It's the same one I had foreseen in my vision.

Halister: "Been awhile since I was brought here. A lot of good folk were with me when I arrived."

"Were?"

Halister: "I don't know what happened to them. One by one they were taken from the cells. Some comrades in arms, some just settlers who had no business being taken with us. If only I were stronger!"

With that Halister kicks in the door to the entryway. It flies off its hinges, crashing through tables and kicking up dust. He needs to become stronger, he says. I beg to differ, watching him launch that door off its hinges. Anyone would revere his strength.

"Relax, Halister. Don't lose sight of the ones we can save now."

Halister lets out a long sigh before stepping into the structure.

Halister: "You're right, Jale, but it doesn't make those we have lost any easier to think of."

In silence we search around in the lobby area of the building. Light beams in overhead from the tattered holes in the ceiling. Several large rocks from the cliff face litter the room around us. Floorboards are not in much better shape than the roof—some have been completely smashed and splintered in hundreds of pieces. The balcony that hung over me in my vision lies collapsed in front of the bar. No trace of anyone on the inside, apart from mugs of alcohol that are strewn about, spilled over in all the chaos.

Halister: "Don't suppose you found any bodies around the place?"

"Nothing over here. I assume the same for you."

He nods back to me, and we both climb over the wreckage back behind the bar. We exit through the gate to the exterior path. Before us, propped against the wall is the very man we have been looking for. His left arm is bruised and bloody, and the other lay broken beside him. The landslide had forced a piece of slate over his right leg, and his ankle took the brunt of the force. Bone probably shattered. No way he is walking on it again if the medical technology in this world is as ancient as the weaponry. Scratch that—even modern medicine would take years to rehabilitate this kind of damage, and even then it may not be possible to heal. From behind the rubble, he slowly looks our way. It startles me to see him still alive. As he speaks out to both of us standing over him, his raspy voice cracks through the dust-polluted air.

Boss: "Halister and—who is your companion here?"

He coughs up a bit of blood, which seems peculiar to me, seeing as how none of the rubble seems to have pierced his chest or stomach. Then I see it—a blade poking out from under the dust-covered tunic. I untie the tunic straps, and removing the garment, the small concealed dagger comes into full view; it had been pushed out of its poorly made sheathe and into him.

Halister just stares into him before shaking his head.

Halister: "Almost feel pity for the man who locked me and my comrades up. Look at this sorry state you're in."

Boss: "Don't pity me. Just end my life, acquit me from this—"

He coughs up more blood before he can finish his sentence. Halister goes to mock the man yet again, but I place my boney arm in front of him.

"I don't mean to deny you your outlet of just anger, but please let him finish."

Halister turns away as he nods back respectfully before pushing himself through the door, disappearing behind it.

Boss: "You . . . will you do me a kindness . . . Take my life and grant me . . . the ending of a fallen warrior . . . rather than a feeble man."

"How would taking your life be more honorable than dying like this?"

Boss: "I'd rather die by a sworn enemy's blade than be . . . taken by . . . the likes of this damned desert."

"Alright, I can't ask you to rest in peace, considering all you've done. But I will grant you this final wish."

Boss: "Thank you . . . reaper."

Drawing the blade out of him, I let it cleave through his freckled throat. The blood spurts out against my skull and hands. I feel it drip off me and into the sand as I drive the knife forward. With his head cleaved from his body, I wrap it with his undershirt, tying it off like a trash bag. Then I stick his knife into the wall behind him, in place of a headstone. Slinging his bagged head over my shoulder, I make my way back outside, where Halister puffs smoke from a pipe into the open air.

"Let's get back on the road. You helped us; time to return the favor. We will meet up with Reina at the entrance of the canyon."

Halister nods.

"Not gonna say anything about what happened back there?"

Halister: "Nothing to say. In a way, I guess I regret not being able to do it myself. But it is done now, regardless of who did it. No one else will be taken against their will to this compound any longer."

"True enough. For what it's worth, I am sorry for stopping you. I just wanted to hear his words till the end."

Halister: "Say anything useful?"

"To me he did. Not sure if it'd be anything you could write home about, though, but it helped me to understand this place a little bit more."

Halister: "This place?"

"Forget it. Let's go."

We shove off toward the gate, and before we can get there something behind us crashes into the ground. Turning toward it, we behold a monstrosity—a hulking humanoid behemoth, each arm as wide as both of us together. In an instant I felt its hostility toward us, and before I can think of what to do, my body reacts. The adrenaline surges through my body as I draw the pistol, firing it for the first time toward the creature. The bullet ricochets off its broad kneecap on its left side.

"You have got to be kidding me."

This thing slams its arm against the side of my body, and I am thrown to the side as if it had swatted a fly. My bones creak from the impact, and I gasp for air, because the wind has been knocked out of me. Suddenly Galahad's voice calls out to me, as clear as day.

Galahad: "Jale, get out of there. Now!"

"Easier said than done, old man!"

Picking myself back up against the canyon wall, I return my attention back to the creature as Halister exhales a great plume of smoke.

"Halister! Run!"

Halister peers over at me. The creature seems to be disoriented from the cloud orbiting it as if it were a mass of gravity. Halister bolts toward me as I stumble off the wall.

Halister: "I'm not leaving another comrade behind!"

"Comrade? You already think of me as a comrade?"

Halister: "Jale, you still have your end of the bargain to keep, so let's go!"

He hoists my arm over his shoulder, and I regain my footing. Making our way past the gate, I avert my head back to see the monster finally wave off the unnatural smoke screen created by Halister.

"What the hell is that thing?"

Halister: "An Unsettled, stronger than ones you normally come across in the badlands. I don't know what the hell it is doing here, though. They normally steer clear of settlements."

The Unsettled beast charges through the wooden gate, knocking over what's left of it and sending the watchtower crashing to the ground.

"It's gaining on us. Can you use another smoke screen?"

Halister: "Not right now. My lungs are on fire from that last one."

"How the hell did you even do that? And where is this thing's head?!"

Halister: "Not right now, Jale!"

Before we know it, the beast's shadow towers over us, and as it goes to slam its arm down, we hear a loud crack, and the whizz of a bullet passes us, embedding itself in the same kneecap I had shot before. The beast topples over as it limps on its uninjured leg toward us, way slower than before. I take my arm off Halister's shoulder, able to support myself again, and as we get to the edge of the valley, Reina comes into view from behind the rifle. A fresh horse is behind her and a wagon full of the escapees.

Reina: "Come on!"

I hoist myself up onto the horse before turning back to see Hallister comically dive into the wagon bed. He regains his balance and grabs the reins, settling the lead horse and taking control. I pull my horse up beside Reina. She climbs on the back and we take off toward the district.

"Where in the world did the wagon and horses come from?"

Reina: "They were already down here when I came. I have no idea. Think Wrath set them up for us?"

"Who cares. Let's get out of this death trap!"

Reina: "Hold up. One last thing: Bring the horse to a stop."

"Stop? Are you out of your mind? You see that thing back there?"

Reina: "Just do it!"

I yank back on the reins as she opens the rifle's chamber and reloads from atop the horse's back.

"Are you aiming for the other kneecap?"

Reina: "No, watch."

As I gaze back over the canyon's entrance, she fires once more, creating an explosion that collapses the entryway. The beast roars in anger, entrapped by the rubble as we make our escape.

"Nice shot! I see you used your leftover explosives to trap that thing in there."

Reina: "I still have a few more, but you're correct."

"Now let's get back home!"

I whip the reins once more, catching up with the wagon that Halister is driving.

12.

DIVINATION

HALISTER: "That thing taken care of?"

Reina: "For now, at least. How the hell did you two attract its attention in the first place?"

"Not sure. I have more questions than you at this point. I can tell you that much."

Reina: "Ask away. Can't guarantee I will be able to answer all of them though."

"We can discuss all that once were back in the district."

With the sun now fully overhead, it takes a lot longer than either of us had planned. To think we would encounter a beast like that. In my past life, you would have had to be insane to ever dream it existed. And with everything I have seen in the line of combat, that is saying quite a lot.

After a desolate ride, alone with my thoughts and the sound of the galloping horses filling the land and the sun shining down hard upon us, the district comes into view at last.

Halister: "Finally, a sight for sore eyes."

"Reina, any place to take the horses?"

Reina: "Most of the mounts are stored just outside the gates. Don't worry about anyone taking off with the horses. The sentries posted around the top of the walls aren't keen on letting that happen."

"What happened to the lawless wasteland?"

Reina: "It isn't law that motivates them. It's respect."

"What do they have to respect us for? Bounty hunters or not, we are still sinners who kill for our own gain."

Halister: "Don't compare yourselves with cutthroats of the badlands who exploit the weak and cull them just for amusement. What the two of you are doing—hunting down these wicked men—it gives people hope, even if only a little."

"Doesn't change the fact we cut the head off a defenseless man and were planning to blow the canyon up from the very start. What if you and your people hadn't survived it, Halister?"

Halister: "But we did, my friend. We survived and have made it here to this safe haven because you and Reina came when you did. If I had to face that monster alone while protecting them, I might not have been able to see the sun overhead again. You may have killed a defenseless man, but you saved my people from that man as well. You are an honorable person, Jale. We are all sinners here, but that doesn't mean we aren't decent folk."

I nod my head as I still think of myself as nothing more than a murderer. Maybe it is for the betterment of others' lives, but it doesn't make it any less weighty on my conscience. In my past life all I did was follow orders. It didn't matter who I hurt, as long as I fulfilled what I had to do at the end of the day. Feels no different than now. The only contrast is I'm starting to grow a conscience about it. I peer down at my skeletal hands. It's ironic: the less human I become, the more human I am beginning to feel.

Reina: "Bring the horse to a stop over here, Jale, I'll hitch the mounts to the posts. Go ahead and show Halister and his people to the guild hall."

"Alright, will they even have a place to stay, though?"

Halister: "We can figure something out for that later. For now let's just get to the guild, Jale."

"This way then."

We pass by the marketplace as my frustrations continue to grow. In all of my years, I have never felt such a strong wave of emotion. I close my fists as we reach the guild hall. I stop and stare down at the sands. My bones rattle and creak louder and louder as the stress builds. Ever since I got to this world everything has changed. Existence is so much bigger than I could ever fathom. I am in a different plane of reality, where things I never even thought possible keep occurring. Monsters straight out of science fiction and folklore, my body stripped down to the bone, people with immense power, the Sins like Wrath able to wipe out an encampment without seeming slightly exhausted. Is this all a dream? Some kind of illusion? It all feels so real. Suddenly I feel someone pull me toward the guild entrance, and I snap back to attention and look over. Fayne is pulling on my glove with tears of blood running down her face.

"Fayne?! What's wrong, are you okay?"

I kneel down as she pulls me into a hug. Habitually I raise my arms to pull her in. As she backs away, she looks up and wipes the blood off her face.

Fayne: "Jale, I'm sorry. I woke up and you weren't there and neither was Reina. I thought—"

"Fayne, you shouldn't be apologizing to anyone. It's alright. We are back now."

Fayne: "I thought I would have to be alone again. Where is Reina?"

I look back toward the gate, through the people shuffling about in the streets. Not being able to spot Reina among the crowd, I pet Fayne's hair as I reassure her.

"Reina will be right back. She had to tend to some things. Come on, let's get you something to eat. You're hungry, aren't you?"

Fayne nods as I take her hand. I feel more at ease now as we both sit down in the mess hall of the guild. Halister and his people sit along bench seats across from us.

Fayne: "Who are they?"

"People we met through the night. Don't worry too much about it, Fayne."

Halister: "Ah, don't be like that to the little one, Jale."

Turning his attention to Fayne, he lets out a hearty chuckle.

Halister: "Me and your pa here are comrades. He saved me from some cutthroats not too far from here. You should have seen him in action. Your pa is mighty courageous and strong."

"I'm not her—"

Reina suddenly leans over both me and Fayne as she brings us together laughing.

Reina: "Yep, all just one big happy family, huh, Jale?"

I sigh as I lean into my hand. If I had eyes, they'd be rolling right about now.

"Suddenly I'm regretting meeting such joyous people as all of you."

Everyone cheerfully laughs as if I had told a great joke. In my confusion I just shake my head, feeling like the joke was at my expense.

Halister stands up and shuffles over to the bar before coming back with several mugs and a small barrel-like thing with a spigot. Filling the mugs one by one, he passes the first one to me.

Halister: "Come now, Jale, it's time to make merry after a daring rescue such as that!"

"It wasn't that great, and besides, I seem to remember having been thrown into the air like a rag doll."

Halister grins. As I raise up the mug, I can smell the alcohol in the drink—must be pretty damn strong. I haven't felt the need to drink anything yet, but it never hurts to see if I can, and on that note, is it even possible for a skeleton to get drunk? I shake my head as I realize how stupid that thought sounds.

"Whatever. All of you can pay for me, one way or another. Down the hatch."

Bringing it up to my mouth, I can actually taste it, and I feel the sensation of liquid entering my strange new body. I look down to check the table and chair to make sure it isn't just going straight through me—that would be embarrassing—but both are dry. It seemingly disappears as I drink. Just like how I breathe without lungs, the way this body works is a mystery to me. Maybe just like that guy's consciousness from before, I am absorbing it into my body. I don't need to understand how I'm able to drink to be thankful that I still can. It helps me hold on to the vestiges of what was once normal.

The drink itself has a very distinct taste, like honey. A mead maybe? Never have been one for drinking, but whatever. I down the whole mug before I set it back on the table. I can feel a buzz come over me, confirming that even if I don't know how, I am certain I am getting drunk.

Halister: "Couldn't even wait for a toast? This man is a hardier drinker than me!"

I let out a laugh as I refill the mug, and we all clash pints together. I look over to Fayne, who is drinking soup broth, and she turns toward me and smiles. Around the table sit those who came with us from the encampment. They seem unfazed, as if everything we had encountered was a distant memory. Others from around the bar come up and sit alongside us, drinking and bantering as if they were age-old friends. This culture, the free spirits of those around me—I admire them. It isn't something I ever thought of myself doing in my old life. Come to think of it, have I ever had a drink with friends at a bar before? I can't recall the last time I was in a bar without a work-related reason. I take in this aroma of alcohol and the cheers and laughter as some guys at the other end of the table strum an acoustic guitar. Another starts drumming on the table, following along to the melody. My mead sloshes over the rim of the mug as more people pound against the table. Reina takes a seat next to me as I raise my mug from the table.

"Feels good to kick back and relax once in a great while."

Reina: "I hear ya, Jale. Listen, don't beat yourself up over these jobs. I can promise you we will try to take any future bounties alive."

Halister: "Rest easy, you're among comrades here."

"How did you know I was stressed?"

Halister: "You really didn't realize how loudly your bones were clunking and grinding. None of us wanted to say anything that could make it worse, then the little one stepped up when no one else here could and put your mind at ease."

Reina: "A few more drinks, and after, there is someone I want you to meet."

"Sounds good. Before that, I want to ask you a question, Halister."

Halister: "Ask away."

"Back there when you inhaled from that pipe, how did you create that plume of smoke?"

Halister: "Ah, that. That is my divination."

"Your what? Some kind of magic? Or are you just pulling my leg?"

The alcohol starts setting in quicker than I anticipated as I push back the empty mug.

Halister: "A divination is, for all intents and purposes, something akin to magic."

"If I hadn't seen it myself, I would pass you off as insane."

Halister: "You would be the crazy one, friend. Not many people in the badlands don't know of the divinations and how they work. Even those who cannot perform them still know of their existence."

"How does it work?"

Reina: "A divination uses an object imbued with your conscience to create or find a catalyst that is then able to be commanded directly by concentration. Halister's pipe is the sourced object, imbued with his own conscience, and the smoke produced is his catalyst."

"I see, so that smoke screen was at your command?"

Halister: "Sadly no, that wasn't even close to being fully under my control."

"What do you mean?"

Halister: "I had just imbued that pipe after I left you with that man. It was a lucky find, but I didn't expect to have to use it so quickly. It was a half-baked divination at best."

"So, if you had full command, you could make it that much stronger?"

Halister: "In my eyes, my smoke doesn't reflect strength, it reflects my adaptability. My smoke can be used in many ways, even some

I probably haven't even thought of yet."

"Are all divinations like this?"

Reina: "No, each has its own strengths and weaknesses."

"What is your divination then, Reina?"

Reina shifts through her bag, pulling out several papers with strings tied around them to keep them wrapped together.

"What exactly am I looking at here, Reina?"

Reina: "Oh, we have to start from there, huh?"

She picks up one of the rolls, pointing to it.

Reina: "This is parchment, made mostly from wild goats roaming the badlands. If not, they're most likely gonna be calfskin."

"Not the material itself. Just tell me how it works."

Reina: "The strings are actually a special material my father developed when he was still among the land of the living. They absorb the essence upon being imbued, and code it to the property of each scroll. These are the most common divinations. It's been determined that, if one cannot harness their ability with these scrolls, they won't be capable of divination."

She hands me a scroll with a clear string on it.

Reina: "Now just focus on imbuing it with your conscience. We will know relatively quickly your skill, as well as whether you could go beyond just simple scrolls."

As I concentrate on the scroll, its rough texture grinds against my hand. Suddenly it starts feeling warmer, as if almost alive.

Reina: "That's it, Jale. Seems like you have a knack for it after all."

The string shifts from clear to pitch black.

"Reina, what does black represent?"

Reina opens a little notepad and flips on through. I then notice everyone in the tavern has gathered around, marveling at the scroll's color shift.

Reina: "Black signifies depths, but the notes my father had that elaborate darker color shifts aren't with me at the moment. They are rarer than that of lighter colors, I do know that. Well, without my father's notes, there's really only one other way to know."

13.
IMBUEMENT

REINA GUIDES US into the back alley of the guild. She pulls me aside while Fayne and Halister stop several yards behind us.

Reina: "Now hold the scroll out away from you and grasp it tightly till the seal breaks."

I do so, and the scroll sets ablaze. I jerk my hand back as the ground splits apart in front of me, as if a small shift in the plates has given way. Sand pours into the severed land, and then a pillar of granite holding two copper rods rises up from the fissure.

"What in the world are these?"

Reina: "They appear to be dowsing rods."

"What exactly does this mean, Reina?"

Reina: "I'm not certain—I told you before I didn't have my father's notes on this. Try imbuing them as you did for the scroll."

After I remove the dowsing rods from the granite pillar, the pillar proceeds to sink back down. It becomes swallowed up by the sands, and they reshape the land as if nothing had happened.

Reina: "Let's see if we can't get a lead to explain more about these later. In fact, after we turn in the bounty I'm sure the guildmaster would like to have a word with you, anyway. Maybe he knows more on it."

"I thought your father was the resident expert on this."

Reina: "True, but just because I am his daughter doesn't mean I'm as skilled or knowledgeable when it comes to divinations. Now, the guildmaster, he worked alongside my father in the study of them."

"Are he and your father on equal terms?"

Reina: "Not quite. Father was an academic at heart. His knowledge surpassed the guildmaster by leagues, even though the guildmaster is no pushover either."

"So more like a student to him?"

Reina: "They taught each other about their own strengths. Dad taught the guildmaster everything he could on the aspects of divination. The guildmaster's teachings were—how do I say this? A bit more brutal."

"Pardon?"

Reina: "While Dad was the expert in the workings of divinations, the guildmaster was our resident expert in practical application of these teachings. Father had studied academics as much as he had trained to perfect his own technique. Speak of the devil himself—"

A man whose hair glistens white in the wind stands before us, and despite his seemingly old age, his physique is impressive. Not quite as built as Halister, but his muscles seem more toned to specific movements rather than raw strength.

Guildmaster: "Reina please, no flattery. You should know there is no such thing as perfection. Even my technique that I have refined over quite a few decades can always evolve to greater heights."

Spoken like a true master of a craft. Even peerless amongst the challengers he has faced, it doesn't sway his pure devotion to honing his skill.

Halister: "Guess that ends this lesson for now. Seems like the guildmaster has some business with the both of you. Jale, me and my people will keep Fayne company. Don't forget to hand over the bounty."

"Right, I won't. Thanks, Halister."

Halister: "Come, little one. I will show you that divinations aren't just for combat. They can be as fun as a festival."

Fayne nods toward Halister, smiling as they both wander off. I face back toward the guildmaster, who extends his hand to me, and we shake as he smiles.

Guildmaster: "We have much to discuss, Jale. However, it'd be quite a bother for you to refer to me constantly as just 'guildmaster.' I am known as Enoch, and I was the one who asked Reina to have you accompany her. For bringing her back safely, you have my thanks. She is like a daughter to me, after her father had—"

Reina: "Guildmaster, I don't wish to have that revealed at the moment. I respectfully ask you to recant your remark."

Enoch: "Apologies, let us just get straight to business then. Reina, please take the bounty to the cellar and collect your payment for the both of you."

Reina: "Understood."

I hand off the wrapped head to her as Enoch signals me to follow. He leads me to a different building. Its walls appear as bricks and its construction is more refined than those that surround it. Yet the bricks have more visible wear and tear. Must be at least a half a century old.

Enoch: "This was where I honed my skill, and it is where I shall teach you yours. It is not my intent to send you or Reina into situations where you require said teachings, however, knowing them at the proper time can save your very lives."

We enter the building; its long corridors slope down and open into a large coliseum.

Enoch: "This coliseum has been here since the district was first formed. It is no longer used as such since I have taken leadership of the district; rather it's used as a training ground for the garrison as well as our bounty hunters."

He steps down from the steeple and into the sands of the arena.

Enoch: "I have always found that the best way for me to train and develop divination was to experience it firsthand myself. Come at me and let me see what you can do. Cast your weapons aside, but feel free to use those rods and as much force as necessary, and if you are capable, your divination itself."

"Alright, then I won't hold back."

Charging him, I grab his arm to bring down his posture and shoot my hand toward his leg. As the sands take him back, he catches my arm then drags me to take my back. Wrapping his arms around my waist, he picks me up into the air before slamming me into the ground. I cough from the impact but roll out of the way as he slams his fist down. I regain position back to my feet before grasping his arm yet again.

Enoch: "Same trick? Jale, you are more experienced than—"

As he is speaking I pull him toward me, causing him to shift his weight. I catch the back of his head before sweeping his leg out from under him, sending him down. As his back hits the ground, the impact causes sand to shoot into the air. Enoch props himself up as he goes to sweep me. I jump back, missing the chance to gain control of his posture.

Enoch: "These aren't just techniques meant for bloodying your opponent but rather to gain the upper hand. You're quite skilled purely in hand-to-hand combat, my boy. In fact, if it were merely that, I believe you'd have me beat already. However, my divination will level the playing field."

Reaching into his dusty overcloak, he pulls out a staff. The end of the staff is fashioned into a crescent moon. He slams it into the ground as the sands start to rise and blow in all directions until visibility is next to none. I can barely make out Enoch's voice through the sifting of the strong sands. How can the wind reach in here, even if he is using his divination to control it?

Enoch: "The first step in a battle between divinations is to analyze the strengths and weaknesses of your opponent's power."

His voice draws closer, and I suddenly feel a strike of his staff against my chest, throwing me back. Somehow, he is able to find me in all this. Even with the strength of my skeletal body, I doubt it's feasible to keep taking staff blows like that for an extended time. The staff suddenly slams against my back at around the same level as where it first struck my chest. I wrap my arm around it, and with the other I reach to pull down on the back of his neck. My hand brushes against him but doesn't quite reach, and I feel his foot slam into my abdomen, sending me down to one knee.

Enoch: "Your skill and combat intuition is frightening."

This time I crouch down below his prior points of contact, and as he swings I feel his staff whir over my head before I lunge forward and take him to the ground. The winds die down and the sand settles back to the earth. Enoch rolls out of my tackle but is left on the ground.

"I knew it. You could tell where I was but couldn't truly see me."

Enoch: "No point in hiding it anymore."

Enoch pulls a long necklace from under his robes, revealing a compass.

Enoch: "I am the first and potentially only person who has this technique. I doubt you will meet another like me in your travels. Jale, I have refined this ability of mine that I dub 'dual imbuement.' My staff, as you have probably ascertained, stirs up and controls the wind to blind you with the sands, and this—"

He gestures with his compass in his hand.

Enoch: "This imbued compass allows me to track the location of those within my winds."

"How long did it take to develop this ability? I have a feeling I have only seen a small fraction of it."

Enoch: "What makes you say that, Jale?"

"You brought me in here not to utilize my strengths, but rather to limit yours. From my understanding of what my divination is, it would work as long as there is sand beneath my feet."

Enoch seems impressed as he nods.

Enoch: "Quite right. I limited the winds I controlled quite drastically. The only bit I controlled was the small breeze let out from my robes when you swept me to the ground. Since then that little bit has been magnified, but I finally lost control the moment you tackled me."

"If you're capable of that much with so little, one wonders what power you would possess in the open land."

Enoch: "Enough speculation about me. Shall you focus on your powers instead?"

"I still haven't the slightest clue how I might do so. It's quite a bit to take in considering how little I know about it yet. Even knowing about it still perplexes me. Truly I can't believe it."

Enoch: "Do you know why the stars are in the sky? Why this land can withstand life even with its harsh climate? What about the very sand you stand upon? How has any of this come to be? The answer is that it doesn't matter. Whether you know the reason or not, you must accept what you may perceive, for that is the only way to move forward. Now stop standing still and focus on those."

He points at the rods tucked into my belt. Drawing them out as if unsheathing a set of blades, I hold them by their ivory-like handles.

"Just imbue them. That's really all there is to it?"

Enoch: "Things must be done in order. Imbuement is the first step in controlling this power. You who have never thought to act by simply believing must find this difficult. Just think of what the depths are to you. What feelings, thoughts, memories, do these depths carry."

I close my eyes and can see nothing but darkness.

Enoch: "Tell me what you see."

"Nothing."

Enoch: "No. No one ever sees just nothing. You just think you see nothing. Even seeing with no light, you see darkness."

"If it's just darkness, then how do I see what lies within it?"

Enoch: "This is where the logical side of you can become an asset. Jale, if you cannot see past darkness in this world, what would you do?"

"I'd light a torch."

Enoch: "Then envision it within your own mind. You control what is within your conscience, no one else. If you cannot see, then set the torch alight so that you may."

As he tells me, I think of times when I had been in underground bunkers. Natural cave formations made into the homes of refugees or military outposts used by terrorists, from my service in the Middle East, from my past life. The rough terrain in Iraq and Afghanistan is not unlike the lands here. These memories come storming back, and suddenly the darkness in my mind dissipates into light as hundreds of torches set ablaze within a seemingly endless cave.

"This is . . . my conscience?"

Enoch: "Finally, it seems you have reached it."

14.

INQUIRY

ENOCH: "Now, from this imbuement, you can see the results. I hope this has given you the resolve to trust in it."

My body starts to feel heavy as I kneel down into the gravel of the cave. I can faintly hear Enoch's voice now as I start to fall into a trancelike sleep. Suddenly I get slammed back against the wall by a strong gale; the wind gets knocked out of me, and standing over me is Enoch with his staff. I regain my breath as I stumble to my feet.

"What was that?"

Enoch: "You were starting to fade into the void of your conscience. You need not go back to that place again for quite some time."

"You had to pull me out of that trance, then?"

Enoch: "Stare too long in the void, the void will start to stare back. This, we believe, is how the Unsettled come to be. They get lost in their own conscience."

"You brought me back. Could you do the same for those Unsettled?"

Enoch: "They are too far gone. Many have tried for years, decades even, that's how—no, never mind. This is where we shall stop for today; it's not wise to keep going after that draining experience for you."

I hold my chest, still in some pain. Enoch starts back up the decrepit steeple, and I follow behind.

"Enoch."

Enoch: "Hmm?"

"I wish to see the full scale of your ability, if I am to face off against people of your caliber or the Sins themselves. I must see for myself what I am up against."

Enoch: "The Sins, eh? Yes, I imagine the full extent of my divination would give you an idea of foes you have yet to face. But now is time for rest. I haven't fought like that in ages. A grand match you were, holding your own, even against my limitations."

"Still though, it isn't enough."

Enoch scoffs as he continues out the arena and back to the coarse streets.

Enoch: "You young ones, always so eager to push forward. I can hardly keep up. See all of this?"

"All of what?"

Enoch waves his arm out toward the rows of buildings that stretch back to the district's surrounding wall. The garrisoned guards look as small as ants from all the way back here. Some of the buildings along the street opposite us are in disrepair, and workers are gathered below. I can smell the smoke from their cigars from here. A strong gust of wind turns their paper blueprints into birds soaring across the sky as they chase after them. I can hear who I presume is the boss cursing up a storm, as if the wind wasn't enough.

Enoch: "The district itself, Jale, all of this has been very taxing on me to maintain."

"You maintain the district? I thought they were Greed's districts?"

Enoch: "This one is not. We house many of the refugees of other districts that are in far worse conditions than our own. Not that it isn't trying to fall apart on me constantly."

We continue back into the guild, and I go to sit, but Enoch stops me.

Enoch: "Come have a drink with me for a bit. We can discuss all of your questions now."

I nod as I push the chair back into place. Up the stairs we start, and before we get into his office I already have my first question ready for him.

"There was a monster at the place you sent us. It seemed as if it had been on a rampage."

Enoch: "Oh? What did this monster look like?"

"It was enormous, standing almost the same height as the houses there, with huge arms. It stood on what looked to be small human legs, but when moving, it used its arms. The pistol's shot bounced right off its knee; the rifle was able to slow it down but not very effectively."

Enoch: "A basilisk. I'm glad to see you survived that encounter. The most egregious part of the situation is how it got there in the first place. Basilisks hate populated areas and tend to steer clear of them unless heavily provoked. Someone lured it there to dispose of the site. I don't know whether it intended to include you or not—more than likely you just happened to be in the wrong place at the wrong time."

He props the door open as I follow him, pondering why it was sent. Maybe to dispose of Halister? Or the people there had out-lived their usefulness? Hearing a stream pouring out into a glass, I lift my head to see Enoch filling two glasses.

"What is it?"

Enoch: "This is a special brew. It had to travel quite a ways to arrive here."

"How strong is it?"

Enoch looks over at me puzzled as he sits and gestures for me to do so as well. As I relax into the wooden chair, I pick up the glass and clink it against his before drinking a bit of it.

"Wait, this is tea."

Enoch: "Well, I am not very fond of alcohol. Doesn't help me to focus. Tea, now that does. How do you know of it?"

"I'll answer your question with another. Where did you find it?"

Enoch looks over his shoulder out a window behind him. The window shutters stretch wide open, revealing a sweeping view of the paths below. One by one, lanterns begin to shine. *Has it been a full day already?*

Enoch: "Sorry, Jale. I don't really wish to answer that one."

"It doesn't really matter to me. Back to the actual questions. How many Sins are there? Do you know of their powers?"

Enoch: "The Sins are numerous. I really have no idea how many there truly are. The ones you are probably referring to however are the seven Grand Sins. Wrath, Greed, Sloth, Gluttony, Envy, Pride, and Lust."

The same as the seven deadly sins from my past life; I wonder if there's a connection? And if so, does that mean Galahad is involved? That being said, I don't remember sins outside of those original seven. Guess it can't hurt to ask.

"So, even more exist outside of the Grand Sins?"

Enoch: "They are known as lesser sins."

"Less lethal than the Grand Sins, I presume?"

Enoch: "That isn't an easy question to answer, in the most general aspect of strength. The Grand Sins would triumph on that margin alone, but lesser sins are not to be taken lightly, Jale. Given the proper circumstances, lesser sins could unseat those Grand Sins. After all, every Grand Sin was once a lesser sin in the past."

"How long have they been around?"

Enoch: "Sins have been around since the beginning of humanity. Only recently have they evolved beyond the cusp of lesser sins. In fact there was no metric to separate the two prior to the first evolution to Grand Sin."

"Has a Grand Sin ever been unseated?"

Enoch: "No, at least not the sin itself."

"What do you mean?"

Enoch: "Those Grand Sins are merely titles bestowed upon individuals of said sin. The individuals have changed over the years, but none of the titles themselves have changed."

Finishing the tea and setting down my glass, I feel more and more relaxed knowing I can finally have my questions answered.

"How does one become a Grand Sin?"

Enoch: "One of three ways: The first, inheriting the title through the death of one of the Grand Sins. It can be passed along to another who possesses the qualities of the Grand Sin themselves—or stolen through killing them. That is the shortest and simplest possibility though. Secondly, as I have said before, a lesser sin may unseat a Grand Sin. Though we know of the possibility, we aren't certain how it is achieved. Finally, the third is merely speculation, and it was formulated by none other than Reina's father."

"Will she mind you talking about him?"

Enoch: "Speaking of him and his research are two different matters."

"By all means, continue then."

Enoch: "The very ascendance of a new Grand Sin, an eighth if you will."

"It has to be possible, otherwise how would the original titles have been created in the first place?"

Enoch: "Precisely the same train of thought as Silas."

"Silas? Is that the name of—"

The door opens behind us. We turn and see Reina.

Reina: "My father? Yes, that was his name."

"Sorry, I didn't mean to pry."

Reina: "It's fine. Dad's work should be shared under his name, anyway."

Enoch: "Reina, care for a drink?"

Reina shakes her head as she leans back against the wall.

Reina: "Continue your questions, Jale. I wanted to make sure the old man here hasn't forgotten anything."

Enoch chuckles as he pours himself another glass.

"Which was the first sin to evolve?"

Enoch: "Wrath was, and to this day, his is the only title which has yet to change to another."

"You mean Solomon has kept the title ever since the beginning?"

Enoch: "Correct."

"When exactly was the beginning?"

Enoch: "I don't quite recall. Reina, do you remember the date?"

Reina: "It was right at the end of the first millennium, century nine, decade seven, year five."

"Nine seventy-five?"

Reina: "Sometime within that year, yes."

"How long has it been since then?"

Reina: "We are in the second millennium now, century five,

decade seven, year three. So we are at fifteen seventy-three now, roughly six hundred years later. In that time the other Grand Sins have emerged."

"I'm surprised you can remember all of that."

Reina: "How could we not? After that evolution, this barren wasteland became commonplace. The stories have been passed down to us from those who witnessed the change. They told us of the world they knew before the emergence of the Grand Sins. Some choose to cower in fear of them, others choose to follow them in honor."

"What about you? And as I asked before, what of their power?"

Reina glares over at Enoch.

Reina: "How long do you plan on keeping him in the dark, old man?"

Enoch holds his empty glass, messing with it before clearing his throat to speak.

15.
REVELATION

ENOCH: "Reina, the map if you would, please."

Reina sweeps everything from Enoch's desk into her arms and sets it all aside. Before returning to the desk, Reina dusts off a chart, then continues to roll it out in front of us. To keep it from rolling back up, four tattered tomes are placed upon the corners.

Enoch: "You asked earlier about the power of each one of the Sins? Of course, not many at this point have not heard of Wrath's capabilities. From the sound of it, you have seen the results firsthand."

"Right. How was he able to generate that much power? Was it a divination?"

Enoch: "I won't get into the specifics of it, but essentially, yes. Wrath's abilities allow him to unleash a great amount of unrestricted adrenaline. The greater his frustration, the greater the power he gains beyond a typical human. Like that of a beast, not unlike the Unsettled you bore witness to."

I nod attentively to let him know I'm listening as I lower my gaze to the floor.

"Go on."

Enoch: "On the opposite spectrum is Greed. He has stayed hidden behind the scenes, building power bit by bit. Honestly, I am not quite sure of his power, but it would be safe to assume he is no pushover. We believe Envy is also working alongside Greed, carrying out his will while he slips around in the dark. Greed and Wrath, as you are most certainly aware, are warring Sins. Greed resides to the north in a district known as the capital. Whereas Wrath resides to the east. He has no base of operations, seemingly always on the move."

"So it seems we have found ourselves smack dab in the heart of a proxy war. What of the other four Sins?"

Enoch: "Pride and Lust have been unaccounted for since their titles slipped from the previous owners. Gluttony is, or at least was, comrades with Wrath for quite some time. I heard he had left his army after Wrath used his army to strike at the very districts themselves. Gluttony understood the hatred between him and Greed. However, he couldn't bring himself to sacrifice others in the name of destroying Greed."

"Seems you're forgetting one: What of Sloth?"

Enoch pauses. With a faint grin and a scoff of laughter, he picks back up the conversation.

Enoch: "Sloth is an old idealistic fool. He is one who wishes to turn the districts from mere slums into sustainable cities. Ones that aren't just a safe haven from the harsh desert, but also from those who would trample over the weak in the name of strength. But to do that he must first destroy Greed's grasp upon them, whilst simultaneously keeping Wrath's army at bay."

"You're joking?"

Enoch: "Afraid not, my friend. I, Enoch, am the Grand Sin of Sloth."

The room seems completely frozen in time as the weight of Enoch's words amplifies tenfold. The man I sit across from is a Grand Sin, not such an easy thought to let lie atop one's consciousness. Eventually I find my words again.

"How long have you been the Grand Sin of Sloth, Enoch?"

Enoch: "Quite some time. To be honest, I don't quite recall myself. Forty? Fifty? Quite possibly even sixty long years."

"Why Sloth though? Seems inappropriate for one such as yourself, who has dedicated your life to honing your divination, wouldn't you think?"

Enoch: "Perhaps a subject for another time. Even I can only speculate, and mere speculation is meaningless."

Reina: "Now that is addressed, Jale, I want to hear your opinion on the current climate of things. We have been hiding in this district for too long. The old man says we bide our time, but for how much longer?"

Enoch: "Until we achieve independence from the capital, then we can—"

Reina cuts him off mid-sentence.

Reina: "This has been the same plan you have had since I was a little girl. Please, Enoch, let me at least hear Jale's input."

Enoch: "By all means, Jale, go ahead."

"I really don't know how dependent the districts are on this capital, much less what it even is."

Reina: "The capital, or capital district, is a place of complete corruption, the source of the slaver and scrapper problems that those of us here in the districts have been facing since Greed came to power. That's why we need to act now, otherwise before long we will all be enslaved. Practically are already."

Enoch: "Reina, that is enough. Jale, there is truth to what Reina says, however, it isn't the full picture."

"Still not easy to wrap my head around all this information, but continue."

Enoch: "The capital lies at the very heart of an oasis. They supply us with fresh food from crops and wildlife, as well as water."

"In exchange for what?"

Reina: "You've already seen it before—the bounties that we collect. They aren't just on humans either, though it seems we have been getting an influx of them recently. Mostly those who have screwed over the capital in some way or another."

"What else are these bounties for?"

Enoch: "The Unsettled monsters that run rampant over the badlands."

"That really doesn't make much sense. Why forsake the districts to slavery, yet provide for them at the same time? You're destroying these Unsettled yourselves. It seems like they need you all to keep the roads safe."

Reina: "We aren't destroying them; we are sending them back to the capital."

"What? Why? What could they possibly want with a beast like that?"

Reina: "Materials."

"You already said the wildlife is abundant in the capital though."

Reina: "Not the traditional materials like leather or rawhide. The very bones of these creatures, along with their blood—these are the materials you see all around us. Jale, did you really think the rifles were made from lumber? Look around this shithole—you see a tree anywhere within any distance of this place? The closest we have ever gotten to seeing one is scavenged picture books from before the Sins."

"You mean everything around us is molded from blood and bone?"

Reina: "Yeah, the ivory from these creatures is extremely dense. I've heard they are stronger than some of the best lumber from the past. Even if there are trees in that oasis of theirs, I doubt they'd rely on them when the supply of ivory and blood is so immense."

"What about the blood?"

Reina: "They have specialists in the capital that refine the iron out of them. Unlike a human being, for some reason, iron is much more prevalent in the blood of an Unsettled. A single basilisk can be drained and refined to yield more than twenty pounds of iron."

"I think I'm starting to feel sick knowing all of that."

Reina: "I didn't believe it the first time I was told, however, my father showed me firsthand in the capital."

"You were at the capital?"

Reina: "Only for a short time. Dad and I fled after the new Greed took power so many years back. Can't say I remember much, or if it would even look the same anymore, but the one thing that was burned inside my mind was the iron refinery. I guess when you think about it, it isn't much different than butchering livestock for meat."

"If you can get past the point that they used to be human. Yeah, I guess after that it isn't quite as disturbing."

Reina: "Well, glad you think so too, cause regardless of what we think, those resources are still valuable in this fight."

"What are you getting at?"

Enoch: "Jale, we would like to request your services once again."

Reina: "That basilisk we encountered the other day, whether injured or not, is still roaming free. We need to slay it and bring it back to the district."

"Just to send it off to the very people you intend to wage war against?"

Enoch: "No, this one is off the bounty list. We are harvesting this one for ourselves."

We? I am not going within a hundred feet of that corpse after we kill it, if I can avoid doing so. I understand why it has to be done, but that doesn't make me eager to see the process itself.

"Alright, how many are going to come along with us to take it down?"

Reina: "Halister already volunteered to help slay it. Him and another hunter, along with you and I."

"Seems a bit light on manpower for that thing. Are you sure we can handle it?"

Enoch: "Almost certain. Be sure to take your dowsing rods along. Never know when you may need them."

"A good soldier knows how to utilize every asset at his disposal to achieve victory, and I don't plan on losing."

Reina: "After we get the haul back, Lanson will take it into his workshop. The capital may have more refiners on hand, but we have the very best one."

"Really? That grouchy old man? Guess there really is more than meets the eye with him."

Reina snickers as I stand up to head back to the tavern to check up on Fayne, after which I'll probably collapse in my bed for a long while.

"Sorry, it's a lot to put on my plate all at once. I need to think a lot of things over after just moving here. Oh, and Reina, I haven't forgotten about your question. Let us take care of this basilisk, so we can all rest a bit easier before I give you my two cents on this war."

Reina: "No problem, Jale. Get some well-deserved rest. You both need and deserve it after that long-winded session."

As I start down the stairs, I can see Halister waving me over already. He's standing at the edge of the table, he and Fayne opposite each other, both with wide grins on their faces.

"Halister, you know she is too young to drink, don't you?"

Fayne laughs.

Halister: "What! You mean to tell me she isn't older than me?"

They both laugh it up as I breathe a sigh of relief.

"Good to have a comfortable sense in the air again at last. Way too stuffy in that room up there, even for me. Also, Halister, I wouldn't have guessed you'd have a way with kids."

Halister: "What can I say, it's a gift, comrade. Now let us get both you and Fayne to your room. Seems like both of you could use it."

Halister guides Fayne ahead of me as I trail shortly behind. We get into the room, and as I hit the bed, I feel my consciousness slip from my body.

16.
DEMONSTRATION

HALISTER: "Jale, time to rise, friend."

After what was more akin to hibernation than sleep, I awake to find Halister shaking my leg. My bones rattle all the way up my spine, and I jerk my leg back as I pick myself up.

"How long was I out?"

Halister: "Long enough. Took a couple of days. Reina and the little lass had been watching over you before I took my shift. You were motionless until just now. Figured if I yelled loud enough to wake the dead, you would come back. Ha! But alas, I didn't want to disturb the neighbors, so a good bone rattle did the trick all the same."

I roll my legs from under the fresh linens, now face-to-face with Halister.

"Guess I just had a lot on my mind."

Halister: "Forget it. Sometimes I find the best way to relieve myself of the worries is to come back around to them. There is only one of you, so don't let your mind do the job of twenty."

"Thanks, Halister. I'll try that."

Halister: "Aye, comrade, get your gear together. We'll meet the rest out by the northern gate. Time to focus on bringing us down a basilisk. This time I won't have to hold back."

Hopping down onto the creaking floor, I grab my belt from a crude nightstand next to the bed. Must have been taken off me at some point. Seems like Reina added a few more pouches while I was out. My arms instinctively reach over my head in a stretch as I yawn and accompany Halister outside to make our way to the gate.

"You were holding back last time?"

Halister: "I thought I told you before—that wasn't the full strength of my divination."

"We shall see if this boast of yours is worth the anticipation."

We get to the north gate after a short trek through town. I'm starting to get a bit used to the layout; it's strangely organized in the outer housing areas. Only problem is the main drag; the back ways are narrow, but the view ranges from one side of the wall clear to the other in the distance. We reach the gate and greet Reina and a youthful looking kid no older than sixteen, who I assume is a friend of Halister's. I can see sweat falling from his ginger hair past the freckles that are speckled across his nose. Reina tosses Halister and me a pair of rifles. They're just like hers, same cartridge. Only difference is the barrels are cut down a good bit.

Reina: "Presents from Enoch. Also, glad you could make it, Jale."

"If I hadn't woken when I did, would you have left without me?"

Reina: "Unfortunately I couldn't stay by your bed any longer; we had a bounty hunter return yesterday. He was sent to track the damn thing—it seems like it didn't take long to break through that rubble after we fled."

"And now it's gone north? Any reason why exactly?"

Halister: "Doesn't matter where it has gone, it all ends with it dead."

"Lead the way."

I tuck the rifle into the horse's saddle holster before pulling myself onto the saddle. Reina snaps the reins of her mount as we ride back into the open desert.

"Does Lanson help fashion the saddles?"

Reina: "Yeah, why do you ask?"

"Not really any reason, just curious."

The rigid leather of the saddle feels just like my cuirass. I wonder if they all feel like this, or if it is just a trait of Lanson's leatherworking.

Halister: "If I recall right, Lanson really is one of the only craftsmen around who knows so many fields."

"What doesn't Lanson do, Hal?"

Halister: "Lanson does anything and everything related to leather or bone. Stocks for rifles, boots, saddles, holsters. Hell, the only thing I haven't seen him work with is metal forging."

"One hell of an asset to the district, despite his demeanor."

Reina: "Lanson cares a great deal about the district, whether he shows it or not."

"Wait. If he can't work metal, how will he refine the iron out of the Unsettled's blood?"

Reina: "Lanson knows how to refine it. Hell, I'd even wager he can do metalwork. I just know he dislikes doing the forgings— more for a blacksmith than a tailor."

Halister: "Look alive friends: Is that not it in the distance?"

Halister's companion shuffles through a black satchel he has hoisted in front his tan vest onto his lap and pulls out a telescope as we come to halt the horses.

Halister's friend: "Yeah, that's the basilisk alright. How are we going to take that thing down with just the four of us?"

Halister: "You doubt us? Think we would set out unprepared for an undertaking? Nay, my friend. As for you, Jale, pay attention, and may you uncover an idea behind your own divination by witnessing mine."

Halister unbuckles a strap covering a hatchet, hoisting it out of the sheath. On the opposite side of the blade, attached to the ax itself, is a hammer-like shape. Only difference is, this one is hollowed out. Bringing it up and tilting the blade edge away from him, Halister holds the end in his teeth as he strikes a matchstick across the rough ax-head and sets alight the tobacco in the pipe, filling his lungs as he inhales from the hollowed-out handle. Just like before, as Halister exhales, he creates a massive plume of smoke. The basilisk appears to notice and moves in our direction.

Halister: "Reina, keep that thing distracted with the others while I finish it."

Reina: "Don't know how much time we can buy you, but alright.

Jale, let's go."

Cracking the reins, I gallop alongside her straight toward that monster.

Reina: "On my mark, pull the reins back and turn. We will keep just ahead of it."

"Understood!"

We get mere moments away from colliding with the beast as she yells over. My horse scampers around and picks back up to a trot directly ahead of the monster. Reina jumps over to my horse, holding a rope connected to the reins of the other as she slips herself back-to-back with me.

Reina: "We need to buy Hal some time, but we have to lure the basilisk to a stop right under that smoke."

Reina pulls the rifle across her body, shouldering it as she fires into the leg opposite the one that had been wounded from before. The bullet sinks in as the creature begins to bleed profusely.

"It didn't do that last time. What did you just shoot?"

Reina: "That shot had more gunpowder behind it than my other handloads for this rifle. Not to mention we are much closer than the last time. It will certainly slow it down, but these things are tough as nails. Its blood will clot rapidly, so it won't be bleeding out anytime soon. Once we get under that smoke I will hit him in the same spot. Let's hope that halts him just enough."

The creature slows only slightly; its leg seals up but the fragmented skin still hangs from its flesh. The other leg looks similar from where Reina shot it before.

"You sure just hitting it again in that spot will be enough? Thought you said you used your best bullet in that shot?"

Reina: "I have just enough to do it. Trust me, this isn't the first time I've had to face these monsters."

"I'll trust in you, then. We are coming up under the smoke now— whatever you need to do, do it now."

Reina: "Pull the horse around beside Hal and stop sideways."

The horse roars as I jerk the reins back, and it slides, kicking up the dust. Reina jumps from my horse as hers follows over, led by the rope. Reina pulls out an ornate-looking crossbow. Anchoring it down with her foot upon the crossbow's hook, she hoists up the string, loading in a bolt with one of her scrolls wrapped around its shaft as the basilisk draws nearer. Just as the creature stumbles under the cloud, she pulls up her crossbow and fires the bolt that is cloaked in the scroll. As the bolt makes impact with the left leg of the beast, the scroll tied to it explodes. With that, the creature lets out an ear-piercing shriek of pain as it tumbles over. Reina reloads her rifle as she yells over toward me and Halister.

Reina: "Jale, get yours ready. Hal, hurry up!"

Halister slings his rifle down to his side as he dismounts his horse. He takes a deep breath as he hurls his ax into the cloud overhead, and a bright flash slams down into the beast. Over the crack of the bolt of lightning I can just barely hear Reina.

Reina: "Get back and fire into it. Make sure it's dead!"

We all shuffle back, shouldering our rifles, and fire in unison. The smoke from the barrels dances up into the air. Our horses, frantic from the commotion, back away from the beast as I slide off the saddle of mine.

Halister's friend: "Is it dead?"

Reina: "After all that, I sure hope so."

"Just in case, reload and let us monitor it for a bit before getting closer."

17.
DUALITY

WITH OUR BOOTS SINKING into the desert sands, we await quietly, watching for the most subtle movement from the slain beast. After a while, Reina calls out to Halister's friend by name for the first time that day.

Reina: "Theo, round up the horses and start strapping the basilisk to the slide for transport."

Theo: "Yes, ma'am."

Theo heads off as the three of us keep our eyes on the beast. The air starts to stagnate with the stench of its blood.

"Will the stench of blood be a problem for Lanson?"

Reina: "Shouldn't. We will know for sure when we get it back to him. Lanson will give us an earful if the—how does he put it?—specimen is fouled."

Halister: "I can practically hear him already. Ha."

"Halister, I've been meaning to ask you this, but it seems like you know some of the people around the district. Have you been there before?"

Halister: "Was my first home away from home, if that makes any sense. I was raised quite a ways west in a different district. However, this district was still the closest in proximity, so commerce naturally brought me here. Specifically the booze, if I am being honest."

"I seem to remember you enjoying it not too long ago alongside me, so yeah, that makes a lot of sense."

Halister chuckles as he nods, while Reina sighs sarcastically.

Reina: "What am I gonna do with you both?"

"On a more serious note, Reina, Halister, your techniques of divination are quite different. Care to explain either of them while we wait for Theo?"

Reina: "Halister, wanna start? You were flashier with yours anyway. No pun intended."

Halister: "Enoch really wanted to wait to tell you, so you don't push yourself beyond your capabilities. Unfortunately, as our situation becomes more dire by the day, with beasts like this roaming about, personally I don't think we can afford to be wasteful of talent like yours."

"Does it have something to do with the Unsettled?"

Halister: "As I'm sure he alluded to already, the void you had to stare into in order to understand your imbuement—it can also stare right back at you, as if peering into your very soul. It's theorized that those who do so are turned into the Unsettled."

Theo marches in front of us, pushing the slide under the beast, and Reina goes to assist. Halister takes the reins of the mounts, handing two of them to me as we hold them steady. He continues on with his lecture.

Halister: "What you haven't been told is that you have not yet finished with that process. Pull out those catalysts of yours."

I hold both straps with one hand as I pull the dowsing rods from my belt with the opposite.

Halister: "Do these look like weapons fit for battle? The answer, obviously, is no. Thankfully, this is the final phase of attaining your divination. If you are curious about the other phases, they go in this order: First connection—this step establishes the nature of your divination and gives you the tools connected with it. Recognition is realizing where the catalyst of the divination forms. Lastly, transformation is the process of refining the tools given to you as a means to engage an opponent."

"Kind of a lot to take in."

Halister: "Sorry about that. You really didn't need the explanation of the other two considering you have already done them."

"How do you know that I've completed the second step?"

Halister: "Enoch wouldn't have brought it up had you not. The final endeavor is the most dangerous among the phase."

"How so?"

Halister: "Really not much of a way I can explain it, like looking into a mirror almost. You will just have to see it for yourself."

"Alright then. Sounds cryptic enough to be a pain."

Halister smirks as we hand off the reins to Theo's and Reina's steeds. We all mount up with the slide straps hooked to our saddles. Setting back out into the open desert, slowly I ride in between Halister on the left, Reina, who shares the center with me, and Theo on the right.

"Come to think of it, if my dowsing rods still have a transformation to undertake, what was the original form of yours, Hal?"

Halister: "A pipe, not unlike the one I used back at the slave camp."

"You use pipes often as a substitute?"

Halister: "It was an on-the-fly decision. I was lucky to have spotted it among the wreckage, and luckier that it worked, even if it did take a toll on my lungs. While you were bedridden, I had to repeat the phases myself in order to reform my hatchet. A lot easier the second time around."

"And what of you, Reina? How does your divination work?"

Reina sighs. As she leans back in her saddle, she shields her eyes as the cruel sun seeks to blind them.

Reina: "The only divinations I have—they're not my own."

"What do you mean?"

Reina: "I don't have my own divination, so the best I can do is redirect others through my scrolls."

"Damn, sounds rough."

Reina: "Well, it isn't easy. Most of the time I can pay to copy divinations from others. Majority of people on the streets would jump at the chance to make a good amount of coin for something that comes as naturally as breathing. Only problem with that is—"

"Finding those who can actually use a divination."

Reina: "Right."

"Follow up question: Are the scrolls usable to everyone like that?"

Reina: "Not quite. If those who don't possess their own divination seek to utilize the scrolls like I do, they'd have several years just trying to understand how to do so. Luckily, my father taught me from a young age how they work. Even though we did not know at the time that I wouldn't have a divination, I still studied them endlessly."

"I have to admire your dedication."

Reina: "I appreciate it, though despite my diligence, these castings are yet to be complete."

Halister: "Don't deceive yourself, lass. If what I witnessed today is not the full potential of these scrolls you wield, well, to put it bluntly, you will become a force to be reckoned with."

"I agree, and if you need a divination for a scroll, I won't charge you a single thing."

Reina: "Thanks. It means a lot."

"The control you already have, it's quick and precise. Even if it isn't as powerful as you desire it to be, there's no doubt in my mind of the sheer versatility these scrolls provide."

Come to think of it, when I first met Galahad, he emphasized the same sentiment. My control of my consciousness was far greater than the power it wrought.

Halister: "They are quite opposite of my divination, the slow build up before a powerful blast."

"Like two sides of the same coin—a duality if you will."

Reina: "Sounds almost poetic, if it didn't bother me so."

As we draw nearer back to the district, I can see figures upon its walls shuffling about. Another is at the gate waving to us. As we get ever closer, it turns out to be Lanson.

Lanson: "Bring it around to the western gate. It won't fit through the north and south, which lead into the residential districts."

Halister nods before we guide the horses around the perimeter and into the west gate. As we enter, folks from all over are gathered around marveling.

Halister: "Reina, where are we taking this monstrosity? It certainly won't fit in any common shop."

Reina: "Oh right, we never told you. It's right over here."

Reina points to a barn-like structure. She waves a red flag over her head as the doors fold outward revealing a huge loft and several people on either side. Benches were filled with tools similar to those I used to see often at butchers for dressing fresh game during hunting seasons. Lanson waddles in through a door leading to the marketplace and cautiously locks it behind him. Gazing back at Reina, I see that she can tell I have a question gnawing at me.

Reina: "They're all craftsmen from nearby districts. Lanson must have reined in a few extra hands."

"Gotcha. Hadn't seen them around the marketplace before."

Craftsmen from either side start skinning the basilisk in front of us. Lanson saunters up to us.

Lanson: "You all, we have our work cut out for us already without gawkers."

Halister: "Quite literally cut out for you."

The four of us share a slight laugh at Lanson's expense as he kicks us from the premises. Without a word Theo steers his steed toward the guild hall. We naturally follow suit, off to report our success to Enoch. As we turn the corner, Enoch is already out front as Theo sprints full speed toward him, lunging forward as if to tackle the guildmaster.

"Oh shit, he's making a lunge toward him!"

In response I draw my rifle, bringing it up to low ready as Reina grabs my arm quickly.

Reina: "Jale! Relax, Theo is Enoch's grandson!"

I stammer, reholstering the rifle and feeling a lump in my throat as I let my head fall into my hands.

"S-s-sorry, I assumed the worst too quickly. Thanks for the quick response, Reina."

Reina: "I get it. A new face rushing headlong toward the most influential person in the district. It would be unnerving to any of us had we not already known. Sorry for leaving you out of the loop. Didn't think it was of any concern."

I sling my leg over the saddle as Halister takes the reins of the horses to lead them out to the hitching posts. Reina follows beside me, linking her arm with mine.

"I feel like I'm losing my damn mind with everything weighing so heavily."

Reina: "Relax, you're too on edge from all the fighting we have been through in such a short period of time. Why don't you talk to Enoch about the last step in the process of your divination."

Letting out a deep sigh, I force out the words behind it.

"Will do."

18.
REMORSE

I'M STILL FLUSTERED FROM MY EARLIER IMPULSE, but I push it to the back of my mind. I gather my thoughts and call out to Enoch.

"Enoch! I need to ask you something."

Enoch: "What is it son? Something troubling you?"

"I'd like to begin the final step in attaining my divination."

Enoch: "Ah, I see that fool Halister ignored my prior insistence that he not mention anything of the sort. Your growth in such a short amount of time is nothing to scoff at. It's unprecedented to see one capable of divination, let alone being two steps into the process, as rapidly as you."

"Even so, I want to become stronger, if not for my own sake, then for my newfound comrades and home."

Enoch: "The task before you is no easy feat, and after just coming back from that hunt, well, I would advise against it. Alas, I cannot hold you from it, daunting though it may be."

"Just show me how, then I will decide myself if I am ready."

Enoch leads us back into the pit of the training grounds as he lays out a tarp and instructs me further.

Enoch: "Rest. Thought. Meditation. One has many ways to understand the path to this last trial. Simply make yourself comfortable on the tarp and picture yourself gazing into a mirror."

I kneel down and adjust myself into a sitting posture as I close my eyes and follow his instruction. Enoch places his palms upon my shoulders, and a feeling of lightheadedness comes over me.

Enoch: "This is the last chance to walk back, Jale. Are you sure you want to continue?"

"I'm ready. Let's get this done, so I can further assist all of you."

Enoch: "Alright then, what do you see in the mirror?"

"Well, it's me."

As the darkness around me starts to clear, suddenly I cannot hear or feel Enoch. Just like before, upon my death, I'm surrounded by a white room. This time, however, a mirror reflecting only myself sits in the center.

Mirror image: "Yourself, you think?"

I jump back from the mirror as my own reflection shatters the glass and steps through toward me.

"What the hell are you?"

Mirror image: "Why, you said it already. I am you, or at the very least, I am part of you. For simplicity's sake, just call me Elaj."

Elaj? Jale spelled backward? He came from the mirror, so it'd be a reverse of my name? Does he think that's amusing?

Elaj: "Just a simple suggestion, nothing meant by it."

The way he speaks is—

Elaj: "Irritating?"

"How did you know those were my thoughts?"

Elaj: "Jale, I've already told you: I am a part of you."

"What part exactly?"

Elaj: "That would be your subconscious. Just as each person has a consciousness, they all have the opposite as well. I know you are familiar with the yin and yang—it's like that. Where there is darkness, light also resides, and light retains darkness as well."

"What's your point?"

Elaj: "You are here seeking power, the next step in your divination."

"Correct."

Elaj: "In that case, you will need me to help you."

"And why is that? I have never used you before. Why now?"

Elaj: "Jale, that is quite rude. You have used me all the time. I am where the thoughts you never speak aloud are sent to, where emotions are suppressed in the back of your mind, where memories are cast into obscurity. That is all me!"

"I don't know how to respond to that."

Elaj: "Simple: remorse. I want you to feel the agony I go through experiencing all that you wish to not. Jale, sit in silence and recall

all that you have forgotten, understand the depths of who you are."

Tears flow out of my eyes uncontrollably. Wave after wave of emotion looms over me—regret, anxiety, rage, despair—as I fall to the floor.

"Stop! Please!"

Elaj: "Why? Do you think you do not deserve to be subjected to such treatment? Get up and face yourself."

I pull back up to my feet, seemingly by my subconscious's will.

Elaj: "You who have known conflict all your life, and even upon death, still seek it out. All this while suppressing the terrible woes it creates. After leaving foreign conflict in your past life, all you did was engage in domestic conflict. When you were reincarnated now into this form, you have ended up right in the middle of yet another struggle among people. Why should I give you a single benefit of the doubt?"

"The conflicts I have faced have been justified. I have given my all in executing orders handed down from—"

Elaj: "What is this? Jale, do you think I do not know what your excuse is for all of this? I have already instructed you to stay silent. I need not hear you, for we are of the same mind. Make no mistake, Jale, this is not a court of law. Justification has no bearing upon the morality of your sins. I know you never thought for a second that benevolent judgment would be something akin to law."

"What would you have me do? Confess my sins then?"

Elaj: "Yes, that's all you must do. You will find the remorse within you far stronger than any form of physical pain."

Moments pass by where I just sit silently in pain as I am at Elaj's mercy.

Elaj: "Mercy, huh? Funny how little you have shown to so many who have crossed your path. I am not blaming you for any of this. I already know, as do you, those who deserved it and those who did not. Those you have struck down, and those who escaped. Jale, you are living out this life the same as the last, and you refuse to see yourself for who you truly are and always will be. That is what makes me the most spiteful toward you. Essentially, that is what makes you hate yourself, because we are one in the same."

"Tell me, what am I refusing to see myself as?"

Elaj: "It has gone by many names: the angel of death, the ferry-man. With your body being made of only bone, maybe the most appropriate is the grim reaper itself. Collecting the consciousness of others, not unlike a representation of one's soul."

"Why are you telling me all this?"

Elaj: "It's so funny to me that without you thinking all of this, I would never be able to tell you in the first place."

"That still doesn't explain why."

Elaj: "It is because, in order to transform your divination, you must transform your thinking. Do you understand why it is called a divination, Jale?"

"You have access to all my thoughts; shouldn't you know my answer to that already?"

Elaj: "In a roundabout way the answer is yes, like a puzzle when you know what the image is supposed to be prior to putting it together. Jale, a divination is called such because it uses your own consciousness as a tool."

"What's so divine about that?"

Elaj: "Do you not recall Galahad's words? Each consciousness given is a fraction of God to every living being. Kind of representative of mankind being created in God's own image."

"And what is your role in this, if you are my subconscious?"

Elaj: "The yin and yang, Jale. Don't forget that without light there cannot be darkness and vice versa. Without evil, there can exist no good. Like two sides of the same coin, like looking into a mirror. They must work together in harmony to offset each other."

"Wait, are you saying—"

Elaj: "Yes, Jale, if consciousness is given as a part of God, then the subconscious must be?"

"Given its place as the devil."

Elaj: "The devil, Lucifer, Hades, Samuel. Just like your titles of reaper, mine are quite extensive as well."

"If you are as you say, then why should I trust a single thing you say?"

Elaj: "Oh, my poor fool of a host, have you not been listening?! I am not just merely the devil, I am your devil, the evil you have in your soul just like every other being has. If you cease to exist, so do I. In order to prevent that from happening, wouldn't you say it is in our mutual benefit to help one another?"

"Not if I am condemned to hell for it."

Elaj bursts out in a sinister cackle before sneering back at me.

Elaj: "You think I am the one to condemn you?! Stop denying yourself. In truth you are practically already a demon yourself. The countless lives you have snuffed out, atrocities committed in the name of some faceless justice. When shall you recognize your true nature?"

"What right do you have to judge me?"

Elaj: "Judge you? No, Jale, you are judging yourself. In your very own words, whether killing in honor or not, you've still taken a life. And what of that boy just minutes ago. You meant to end his life without mercy. Jale, you are your worst critic. After all, even me saying all this is just you having a mental breakdown inside your own head."

"Then what would you have me do?!"

Elaj: "That is so very simple, Jale. I want you to recognize your faults and stop pushing your emotions upon me. Your addiction to fighting—all you need to do is recognize it. That remorse you keep feeling is simply a symptom of withdrawal. Lastly, you must stop fighting without purpose, not just at the behest of another's orders. That is your greatest sin, for you are the banality of evil, allowing those whom you have never known to use you in spreading that evil."

"Just let me go. Free me of this dread."

Elaj: "Jale, free yourself. Wake up and consider my advice. Until then, you will never allow yourself to perform a divination."

19.
CREATIVITY

I WAKE UP with my head pounding, as if it had been slammed against a concrete wall. I gaze at my surroundings, finding the familiar pit of the training grounds. As the pain subsides, I notice Enoch's absence, and in his place stand Reina and Fayne.

Reina: "You okay? Seems like that was rough."

"Is it that obvious?"

Fayne: "Are you going to be alright, Jale?"

"I think so. Don't worry yourself for my sake, Fayne."

Reina: "She seems to care a great deal for you. I don't think it would be an option for her not to at this point."

"Guess you're right there."

Reina: "Well, how did it go?"

"If I had to guess, poorly."

Halister calls out as he overhears us speaking.

Halister: "What?! You, Jale, of all people, weren't able to attain it on your first try?"

Reina: "Don't be so naive, Hal. You couldn't do it either. As for me, mine will never be complete."

Halister: "Sorry, it's just that, of all people, I would have thought Jale would have done so in one fell swoop. So, what did it say, friend?"

"Something to the effect of recognizing who I am. Otherwise I won't be able to allow myself to cast a divination."

Halister: "Staying true to yourself then? Sometimes it can be hard to sum up what those things are trying to tell you. They speak in riddles, and not all of what they say should be followed, though there are lessons you can only be taught by yourself."

"Look who is speaking in riddles now. If you don't mind me asking, what did they say to the both of you?"

Reina: "Mine told me to convince myself of my strength—kind of hard to do so with how limited I feel. When just the method of my incomplete divination took years to form. Let alone how difficult it is to pull it off."

Halister: "And that is why yours will stay incomplete. The very concept of that kind of meditation is to reform how you see yourself. Only you can hold yourself back."

"Halister, not to change the subject, but what of yours?"

Halister: "Quite the opposite of Reina's. In order to achieve the strength I sought, it told me to recognize how weak I am."

Halister helps me to my feet as we start up the steps to the outside. Before we even reach the second step, I notice Fayne standing still behind us.

"Fayne? Are you alright?"

Fayne: "Well, you told me to tell you what they said, didn't you? I thought you might want to hear mine as well?"

Reina: "Fayne, what did you just say?"

Halister: "The girl has gone through the divination process?"

Fayne: "Sorry, it seemed like something I would need if I wanted to fight alongside you all someday?"

Halister: "How did you even know how to do so?"

Fayne: "I have been watching each time. It wasn't easy, but during the time you all have been gone, I was practicing it."

Halister: "That's astonishing, little one. If you don't mind, show us what power you wield."

Reina kneels in front of Fayne and hands her a scroll.

Reina: "You know how to imbue it then, if you made it this far, don't you?"

Fayne: "Yes ma'am."

Reina: "Just Reina is fine, Fayne."

Fayne nods as she takes the scroll in her palm and begins to imbue it. The scroll's color turns from clear to a dark blue, reminiscent of sapphire.

"Reina, what does this color mean?"

Reina: "This shade of blue is the representation of the cold, whether it be air, water, or even rarer, snow and ice. With it she can utilize them at her will."

"Rather a difficult thing to do in this wasteland, don't you think?"

Halister: "Oh, I wouldn't be so sure about that."

"How do you figure?"

Halister: "Just because you're out of your element doesn't mean you cannot harness it. For me, the clouds above us I will never reach, and so, with my pipe in hand and a breath from within, I can make my very own clouds down here on the surface."

I notice the flask pouch upon Halister's belt as he shifts his posture.

"I wonder, Halister. Hand me your canteen there."

Halister unstraps it and tosses it my way as I snatch it from the air and pop the lid.

"Fayne, clasp your hands together."

Fayne nods as she does so, and I fill her hands with the water. At first drop, the water begins to form small flakes of ice within it. They form faster and faster, and before long the ice begins to rise into the air.

"What the?"

Halister: "What were you trying to do, Jale?"

"I just wanted to see if it would cool or freeze. I hadn't expected this."

Reina: "Look, you two, the ice is forming together."

Fayne marvels at her hands as the ice sculpts itself into a small pick about a foot long. The bottom hardens into a sharp edge as the top forms the head of a hammer.

Fayne: "Woah, amazing!"

Reina: "Jale, just as your divination formed your dowsing rods, Fayne's has done the same in the form of this hammer."

"An ice pick, literally made from ice."

Halister: "Well, little one, what all can you do with that pick?"

Fayne grasps its handle with her bare hand as she curiously points it toward the flask. The water flows out and spirals around the handle of the pick. Halister takes out his hatchet and breathes in the smoke from its handle. Upon exhaling, the smoke forms into the shape of a person on the other side of the training grounds.

Halister: "Swing that pick of yours toward my smoke figure in the distance there, little one."

Fayne pulls the pick back, and as she brings it down, the water silently speeds through the air, freezing into an icicle before splitting the smoke apart and shattering against the solid wall.

Reina and I stand in shock as Halister chuckles and lifts Fayne onto his shoulder as she giggles in excitement.

Halister: "Aha! This little one—no—Fayne! You will surpass even the three of us in no time at all!"

Reina: "Good grief, it was already a hell of a feat to manage the final transition of the divination at her age. Let alone being able to utilize it this quickly."

Halister: "I will tell you the same thing I told her, comrades. Thinking too hard can burden your mind. Just think like a child. Maybe it's as simple as that, after all, and because she is a child, it isn't difficult for her to think as one."

"Fayne, earlier you mentioned that entity said something to you as well. What was it, if you don't mind me asking?"

Fayne: "It came to me in my dream, actually."

"A dream? Not like how I just was?"

Fayne: "Correct. In that dream, my reflection appeared in the lake I had been gazing into. Before long it started to move all on its own as it came out of the lake and stood over me."

Reina: "What message did it convey to you?"

Fayne: "It insisted I not be idle as I am now, but keep moving forward despite my fear. I know it sounds weird to say it like this, but even though it was my reflection, it felt like my mother or father was doting on me. In a way, it comforted me to be guided forward like that. But from the way you all spoke, it seems my experience was far more pleasant. Should I not have said so?"

"No, it's fine, Fayne. I think I speak for all of us when I say we are happy to see you grow."

As Hal sets her down on the ground, I reach my hand out, patting her head as Reina passes by us all.

Reina: "If Fayne's being told not to sit idle, we shouldn't either."

"I still have a few questions, but you're right, I will ask on the way. Wait, where exactly are we going?"

Reina: "Always the inquisitive one, aren't we? Back to Enoch. We should report the progress you and Fayne have made."

"Wouldn't exactly call that progress."

Upon exiting the building, I hear Galahad's voice once again.

Galahad: "Jale, at last I can reach you once again."

"What do you mean?"

Reina turns around with a puzzled look on her face.

Reina: "Who are you talking to, Jale?"

"Oh sorry, it's nothing. Just thinking out loud."

Reina: "Maybe that divination really was too much for you. You're muttering out loud like Lanson after he's served someone at his shop."

She smirks as she pokes fun at me. In response I just shake my head and continue listening to Galahad.

Galahad: "Where exactly were you? Are you alright, Jale?"

Suddenly the very familiar voice from the mirror chants back at Galahad.

Elaj: "Of course he is alright, you old fool. I merely gave his psyche a slight pinch. Not anything to leave a permanent scar."

They are like an angel and devil sitting upon my shoulder. Great, that's just what I need right now, to look like a psycho talking to himself.

Elaj: "It isn't polite to refer to Galahad as a devil, you know?"

As if. You clearly know I was thinking of you. Wait, can you hear my thoughts?

Galahad: "Yes, dear boy, it seems true that we can hear your mind."

Galahad, what did you mean that you can reach me?

Elaj: "That would be my doing, Jale. Wouldn't have wanted this stubborn geezer to interrupt our meeting."

Both of you are occupying what little sanity I have left.

Galahad: "If you wish not to hear us, then you can block both of us out, however, you cannot hear us independently."

Elaj: "That's correct, Jale. You either heed either you heed our word or silence us both. No volume control to pick and choose."

The choice is obvious to me then: Both of you be gone!

Galahad: "Understandable, Jale. Call upon me if you ever seek advice. Just know if you do, this heathen will be alongside me."

Elaj: "So boring. What is a little insanity but to spice things up. May we speak again, Jale."

With that I wait for a few minutes, seeing if they are truly gone, as we continue back to the guild. I hear nothing but silence as we walk. Finally, silence once more.

Reina: "So what was it you wanted to ask, Jale?"

"Oh sorry, it slipped my mind. I'll let you know if I think of it again."

Reina: "No problem."

20.
PERCEPTION

Mystery voice: "No no no, I have told you time and time again, we will leave ourselves open if we act too hastily."

A voice rings out in a room down the hall from Enoch's office.

"What's going on in there?"

Reina steps in front of me as she opens the door to the office. Seeing no one behind the desk, Reina turns her attention back to me.

Reina: "Well, I would have liked to ignore those in that room, but unfortunately it seems unlikely that we can. Enoch is in there with them I would imagine. If no one intervenes, they could be at it for hours."

Reina leads the way. She knocks on the door, and a man in a guard uniform opens the door for us to see two elder men opposite each other at a table. The table itself has a huge map of the surrounding area with several question marks and symbols littered across it. Between the two, at the far end of the table sits Enoch, simply letting the two of them argue with no restraint. One of the men wears a similar uniform to the guard that had allowed us in, only difference is the shoulder markings. Perhaps a high-ranking officer of the guard? Behind his glasses are weathered, baggy eyes. The dark circles fade down to his cheekbones, which are wrinkled into a frown. The man opposite him, appearing nearly just as aged, wears a humbler outfit. Definitely not military, more of a civil servant kind of air about him. Unlike the elder in uniform, his face is gruff with a jagged stubble. He bears wrinkles just as the other, but his are like leather pursed up from conditioning. The two of them stop to meet our intrusion with scowls.

Elder in uniform: "I told you to send your people notice not to interrupt us."

Gruff-looking elder: "As if I care what you tell me. And besides, these aren't my people. Probably more of your guard, coming to check whether you bit the dust yet."

Elder in uniform: "Is your vision failing you now, too, you senile scoundrel? They can't be mine, dressed in no uniform."

Enoch stands from his chair, clearing his throat.

Enoch: "Reina, Halister, Jale, and Fayne, please come in and close the door, friends. We are just beginning to have a nice meeting to plan for the future."

The two elders look baffled as they turn back to Enoch.

Elder in uniform: "Sorry for my rudeness toward your guests, Enoch, sir."

Gruff-looking elder: "Forgive my barking, Enoch, sir."

Enoch: "I require no apologies. In fact it is quite amusing to see the two of you bickering. Though maybe you should offer your condolences to our guests in substitution for me."

They lower their heads respectfully toward us as we enter. They don't seem like the type to do something like that commonly, so it throws me off guard. Enoch must retain quite a lot of respect and admiration from the both of them.

Elder in uniform: "Guards, we have the company of Enoch now in the room. Please station yourselves outside the door and make space for them."

The two guards take up their rifles, nodding as they leave us.

Gruff-looking elder: "Now that your lackeys have cleared out, I suppose some introductions are in order."

Elder in uniform: "It's as you say, very well. Guests of Enoch, I am Commandant Callaghan of the district guard. Pleased to make your acquaintance."

Gruff-looking elder: "The name's Garrett, head of the department of commons. Nice to meet you folk."

Commandant Callaghan: "As unrefined as always. This is the problem with you, Garrett. If you can't even handle introductions, it is a wonder how you have handled your department thus far."

Garrett: "Yeah? Well, I say the reason people around here ain't given the time of day is because of your pompous refinement. You ain't connecting to the people up on your high horse, friend."

"Enoch, they always like this?"

Enoch laughs as the two lower their heads to the board.

Enoch: "Actually these two have just recently developed to this point. The stress of having a war at our doorstep along with maintaining their current duties will do that to leadership."

Reina: "With all due respect, sir, how can you be laughing so casually when they are like this?"

Enoch: "Because it shows me how much they truly care. Had they not ever argued over anything, I'd be more concerned with the level of responsibility they are taking, or worse yet, that they have no compassion for the people of the district whatsoever."

Enoch takes a long sip of tea, the room now silent as we hear the audible slurp from his lips. Breathing out a satisfying sigh, Enoch begins to speak once more.

Enoch: "Now, clearly you haven't come here for the express purpose of meeting these two. What say you, Reina?"

Reina: "Sir, we have some developments regarding the divination attainment. Jale's meeting within the trance did not yield results, however, it also did not bar him entirely from achieving them."

Enoch: "Not much of an update then."

Reina: "Well, sir, you see, Jale wasn't the only one trying for the attainment of a divination."

Enoch: "I beg your pardon? Who else has done so?"

Fayne steps forward toward Enoch as she picks up the teapot. As she begins to pour some out into a cup, the stream freezes in place.

Enoch: "What!? This child has . . ."

The faces of the elders around the table turn to pure amazement. This little girl has pulled off a feat at such a young age that many are never able to. Reina doesn't falter in light of this and continues on.

Reina: "Yes, sir, it seems that under our noses, Fayne was practicing to become stronger by attempting the attainment of a divination."

Enoch: "Seems she did far more than just attempt it. This is astonishing. Halister, did you put the little one up to this?"

Halister: "No, sir! I never had such intentions. I did tell her a lot about the divinations, but I never would have thought she'd take matters into her own hands."

Enoch: "Well, it seems you aren't a bad teacher, if that is the case. Can I ask you to mentor the little one in my stead? I have much to do unfortunately, so I cannot step away, but this is great news. Just assure me you will monitor her progress going forward."

Halister: "It would be a pleasure, sir, thank you. Come, Fayne, it can't be too comfortable or exciting to be cramped up in here listening to the rest of this meeting. Let us celebrate your achievement, little one!"

Halister and Fayne retire to the lower lobby, leaving Reina and me with the elders. It seems Halister is never one for this kind of stuffy atmosphere. Can't say I blame him either.

Enoch: "Jale, please forge ahead with your own attainment. I know it may sound contradictory to what we have just witnessed, but it is not so easily done."

"I know. I am not so low to envy Fayne's abilities. I'm happy for her to not have to go through as rough a time as others."

Enoch: "You have a good heart, Jale. I admire that. Now back to the argument at hand."

"Yes, what exactly seems to be the issue here? Also, I hope you both don't mind answering any questions I have about the matter."

Commandant Callaghan: "As long as the answers may be given at Enoch's discretion."

Enoch: "Jale is a trusted ally now, Callaghan. Reina has vouched for him, and Halister has taken quite a liking as well. I see no problem with answering anything at this point."

Commandant Callaghan: "Understood, sir. Then I will begin by explaining my position."

Callaghan points out our positioning on the map as well as the whereabouts of the capital far to the north.

Commandant Callaghan: "At the moment we are deadlocked between Greed's forces, our own garrison, and Wrath's army. Taking the fight to either side leaves vulnerabilities that shall be exploited by the opposite party."

"Do we have any advantages?"

Garrett: "With the amount of districts there are, Greed and Wrath have no idea which one houses our faction."

"Is that it?"

Commandant Callaghan: "Unfortunately, it is."

"So why were you arguing, exactly?"

Garrett: "Well, your pompous general over here wants to send out small units to both our adversaries and thin down their numbers, if given the opportunity."

Commandant Callaghan: "It's better we act now than cower behind our garrison, waiting for the two of them to trample over us."

Garrett: "It's too risky. Not only that, but we would leave the garrison here weak. Not to mention what will happen if they track them back to this district. Forget about being trampled. They'll starve our people out. You seem to forget that we are still reliant on the capital for the food that feeds your guard and my workers."

Commandant Callaghan: "Won't be any mouths to feed anyway if we get stamped out before we make a single move."

Reina: "Thus, there's a deadlock not only between the three factions, but between the elders as well."

"Enoch, what say you?"

Enoch: "I am not here to promote my thoughts, merely to moderate."

"It definitely isn't a great position to be in, however, a fresh set of eyes can make a great difference when it comes to strategy. Reina, remember when you asked me what my thoughts were on this very matter? Well, now is the time to start taking notes if you'd like."

Commandant Callaghan: "Something we aren't seeing?"

"Right. Not that I can blame either of you. Things are different when you are actually out in the field rather than behind a map. First off, you said you were in a deadlock, right? Well, even if that is the case, it's the same for your adversary as well."

Garrett: "That's true. I hadn't thought of it from their perspective. They make a move on us, all the same, they'd be left vulnerable."

"There's one piece that just doesn't add up to me in the grand scheme of things."

Commandant Callaghan: "That being?"

"What is the status of Wrath's army?"

Commandant Callaghan: "What do you mean, Jale? They are moving like normal."

"Moving?"

Commandant Callaghan: "Yes, they're nomadic, moving from place to place."

"How many districts do they go through? Were they headed anywhere specific?"

Commandant Callaghan: "None that I have heard back from. The traders coming into town would often report them out east, but if they came upon a district they would likely pillage and destroy it. That is Wrath's end goal anyway, being at odds with Greed."

"It seems you've all been fooled then."

21.
CLARITY

COMMANDANT CALLAGHAN: "Are you questioning our intelligence, boy?"

"No, I mean no disrespect."

Garrett: "Then what exactly do you mean? Don't think either of us like the idea of being called fools, and we don't agree on a whole lot."

"The information you have been getting is off. Where exactly do you attain it?"

Commandant Callaghan: "It comes in directly from the guard after statements from travelers or refugees from other districts."

"Refugees?"

Garrett: "Right. That's another problem we've been having lately. With the destruction of districts by our mutual friend, Wrath, we get an influx of people from them looking for work. The problem is we've already delegated every job that doesn't require a specific skill set. Mostly menial labor and the like. You may have seen these refugees in the streets. We don't like leaving those who come to us for help out to dry, but we have our hands tied."

"And you wouldn't think these refugees would have a bias against the people who destroyed their homes?"

Garrett: "Excuse me?"

"The information you are getting about Wrath's goal of destroying the districts is coming from people who have had it happen to them directly."

Commandant Callaghan: "Your point?"

"You think they don't bear grudges against them, triggering them to come to conclusions out of ill intent? I'm not discrediting their suffering, but imagine if you will, someone comes and holds you at gunpoint. What would you gather from that information alone?"

Garrett: "That they intend to kill me?"

"Right, but do you truly know their family isn't starving? Do you know whether or not they have any other option? Like I said, I'm not defending these actions, however, the afflicted may not see past the anger they feel to discern the motive behind these attacks."

Garrett: "That's purely speculation though, isn't it?"

"It is, but if we were to assume the goal of Wrath's army was to wipe out the districts, what is stopping them from steamrolling over them?"

Commandant Callaghan: "Greed's forces, of course. If they move rashly, they'll encounter them."

"See, in hindsight that does make sense. However, how long does it take for the garrison of each district to report directly to the capital?"

Commandant Callaghan: "That's . . . at least a two-day trip there and back. It wouldn't give enough time to dispatch forces."

"So I ask you my question again, why not steamroll through the districts? By the time Greed's forces would be able to get to any of them, Wrath's army would be out of the area with no trouble. Not only that, but with the refugees leaving in every direction for other districts, they'd be nearly impossible to track. Also, if Greed split his forces and tried strengthening the garrisons, they'd be able to selectively pick them off one by one with proper planning. It isn't a great position for Greed to be in. Makes me wonder why he would allow himself to be put in such a position at all."

Commandant Callaghan: "Then what are Wrath's true intentions?"

"That is the golden question now, isn't it? There has to be some reason for the attacks on specific districts. Beyond that still is the question: What are the districts to Greed? Doesn't seem like he is all too amped to defend them."

Commandant Callaghan: "You said it yourself, didn't you, Jale? Splitting his forces to strengthen the garrisons would leave them spread out and therefore less effective in the face of Wrath's whole army."

"Right, but even so, that would be a better option than letting them fall."

Reina: "Could it also be that Greed is cautious of us?"

"Maybe, but if we were provoked so easily it would draw out his forces to stamp us out in one fell swoop."

Reina: "Enoch, sir."

Enoch: "Yes, don't think too hard on it for now, Jale. You have conveyed enough in this meeting."

"Are we adjourning then?"

Enoch: "For the time being, yes. There is a new task, though, for you to carry out."

"That being?"

Enoch: "Well, as you put it earlier, all this talk of Wrath's true intentions toward the districts is mere speculation. Jale, wouldn't you say it would be better to hear directly from the man himself?"

"You want me to track him down?"

Enoch: "Precisely."

"And what do I do once I find him, if I am able to."

Enoch: "Simple, I'd like you to invite him here."

As the words leave his lips, both Garrett and Callaghan stand in unison, protesting Enoch's request.

Commandant Callaghan: "Sir, you mustn't jest with us so."

Garrett: "Bringing Wrath—the very man who has destroyed other districts—here? Even with all that's been said, it is no confirmation that he won't do the same here."

Enoch: "I respect the concerns you've both shared, however, Jale will be asking Wrath on my behalf. Do you understand, Jale?"

It takes me a moment to understand what he means by that. Before long, it clicks.

"You sly old fox, you're guaranteeing his cooperation."

Garrett: "Care to explain what you've graciously discovered, Jale?"

"If I am able to track him down, extending a mere invite back to this district wouldn't garner much attention. But asking at the behest of the Grand Sin of Sloth will elicit a different response. To imply that a man as powerful as a Grand Sin is able to track Wrath down isn't going to sit well with Wrath. We would have the advantage of knowing his location."

Commandant Callaghan: "But we don't even know his location now. How would we track him a second time?"

Garrett: "Ah, I understand. It's a bluff. We won't actually know where he would be heading, but implying that we can will force him to cooperate with us. At the very least he would have to recognize the possibility of having two Grand Sins stalking him."

Commandant Callaghan: "Right, and rather than taking that risk, it'd be wiser to form a pact. The enemy of my enemy is my friend."

"On top of that, he won't be able to topple this district so easily with a Grand Sin stalling his retreat. We'd be able to keep tabs on him if he attempted to do so but also reveal ourselves to Greed. If two Sins fought, it wouldn't be unlikely for people to flee to the capital and report the disturbance. Mutually assured destruction is your game—that about sums it up, Enoch?"

Enoch: "I'm not sure what you all are on about. I am simply asking an acquaintance to talk over tea."

With a smirk he nods to all of us as we get ready to set out. Before we do, I ask one final question of Commandant Callaghan.

"Commandant, where is the person who drew up this map?"

Commandant Callaghan: "Should be around the office of the guard, why?"

"If possible, I'd like to request their aid in tracking down Wrath."

Commandant Callaghan: "I understand, however, I cannot lend him to you without proper instance from the guard itself."

"Meaning?"

Commandant Callaghan: "I need a more official reasoning behind the request. Otherwise, the men may question their stations."

"You mean the men of the guard may want to be dispatched as well. In that case, while we are out there, we will also be updating the map itself. Think of it as a scouting mission, listing it as such rather than as the tracking of a high-profile target like Wrath won't turn any heads."

Commandant Callaghan: "Very well, I will have them rendezvous with you and whoever else you are taking tomorrow at the northern gate at dusk."

"Thank you, commandant."

Commandant Callaghan: "If it means securing the future of the districts, it is my pleasure."

Reina and I lead out of the meeting, heading back to the rooms. We pass Halister and Fayne sitting at a table in the guild's tavern. Halister remarks as we walk by.

Halister: "Quite a long meeting you both had in there. Too much for a simple man like me to wrap my head around. Care giving me the overall verdict?"

Reina stops in the entryway to the rooms, leaning against it.

Reina: "We set out tomorrow at dusk. Will we be seeing you with us?"

Halister takes a long pause before shaking his head.

Halister: "No, you both heard that I am entrusted with Fayne's instructions. Now you both get some rest. Going to be a while before you make it back here. Dusk of tomorrow will be here quicker than you may realize."

"Thanks, Halister. Take good care of Fayne while we are away."

Halister: "Of course."

We both retire to our rooms. I'm left alone once more staring at the ceiling as I lay awake upon the bed. Before long, my head starts to feel light, and I drift into a serene sleep. One I had haven't had in what feels like years.

22.
HIGHLANDER

I AM AWAKENED BY A SOUND LIKE shattering glass. Sitting upright, my back against the headboard of the bed, I listen. Peering over to Fayne's bed, I find it empty. The shattering noise rings out again.

"What is going on outside?"

Gathering my gear and slinging the rifle that I leaned between the wall and nightstand over my shoulder, I shuffle out the door to investigate. It doesn't let up as I head down the hall and out into the sandy streets, the morning sun blinding my vision as I emerge from the guild hall. With the sound echoing around me, I surmise it to be coming from up the alleyway. Heading in that direction, the sound gets louder, and I can hear a muffled voice but can't quite tell who it is or what they are saying. As I come closer and turn the corner, exiting the alleyway, I can see Fayne and Reina standing opposite each other.

Reina: "Alright Fayne, one last time. Are you ready?"

I watch curiously, wondering what they are doing, as well as what they did to cause that noise earlier. Fayne nods her head as water gathers around the pick hammer. Swinging it toward Reina, the water solidifies to ice and speeds toward her like an arrow.

"What the hell are they up to?"

Reina takes a defensive posture and unwraps a scroll. She flings it in front of her, and the parchment spreads out finely as if being slammed against an invisible wall. Suspended in midair, the ice beams into it and shatters, revealing the sound from earlier. Suddenly, I hear Halister talking to my left. I hadn't noticed him leaning against the side of the building.

Halister: "Reina is prepping her divination for the long trek you'll be on. It was actually my idea to have her take some of Fayne's power along. It also gives Fayne a bit of practice with her abilities."

"How long have they been at this?"

Halister: "With just Fayne alone, I would say roughly an hour. But that wasn't the only divination she collected."

"Your smoke as well?"

Halister: "My smoke, as well as the lightning I showed when we took down the basilisk. She also has a single scroll of Enoch's wind."

"Can't believe someone with that versatile of a power doesn't think of herself as strong."

Halister: "It is because of the trade-off in power. She can't turn a divination around and use it in the same manner or level of power, and doing it wrong can quite literally blow up in her face."

"Not in the same manner? What do you mean by that? I understand the power trade-off, but why the lack of similar use?"

Halister: "Well, for example, my lightning comes from the sky above after producing a cloud. When she casts that same ability, she will not be able to get a scroll that high into the air, so the way she will have to position its attack pattern is more like a straight bolt of lightning. That being said, none of us know how exactly that will act with the sands as a ground. Will it latch onto anyone nearby or just the straight target? Aiming it will be quite difficult without knowing the trajectory of the arc."

"How does she plan to go about using it?"

Halister: "She has that crossbow of hers as well. With that, it is possible to determine the trajectory before ever activating the scroll."

"That's kind of funny, in a way."

Halister: "Why's that?"

"Either way, she will be using a bolt of lightning."

Halister: "These jokes of yours are terrible, friend."

Halister snorts out a slight laugh as he starts walking past me.

"You laughed, even if only a little. I still got it out of you."

Halister: "Fine, you win. It was amusing."

Halister turns back and waves to Fayne. Both her and Reina head toward us. Fayne politely nods toward me before taking Halister's hand, who guides them down the alleyway. Turning my attention back to Reina, she lets out a deep sigh after stretching her arms up.

Reina: "Ready to get a move on?"

"Seems you've been waiting eagerly."

Reina: "I wanted to be prepared for anything, so I'm taking as many scrolls as I can carry and my best equipment with me."

She picks up her gear off the ground in the spot beside where Halister was leaning. It is the same scoped rifle from before, but her belt has more pouches and a heavier satchel at the very back. She notices me looking as she straps it on.

Reina: "Getting an eyeful?"

"Oh sorry, that wasn't my intent."

She playfully punches me in my shoulder and my bones rattle from the impact.

Reina: "I know, but I gotta mess with you sometimes, Jale. Wouldn't be any fun for me if I couldn't jest."

"Let's head out then. We won't be able to make our comedy debut standing here."

Reina and I drop by the guild and say our farewells. Before heading to the gate, we stop into the marketplace. Reina packs a bag with many dried meats and slings it over my shoulder for me to carry. She leads us back to Lanson, popping in to find out how the processing of the basilisk is going. Lanson is snoring at the front desk he has set up as a store counter.

Reina: "Lanson? Lanson? Wake up, you old coot!"

Lanson jolts awake, snapping back at her as normally as if he'd been wide awake the entire time.

Lanson: "What are you doing in my store. We are closed!"

Reina: "Says the one not locking up the front door. So how is the basilisk coming?"

Lanson: "It's a chore as it always has been! None of you youngins understand the stress and work me and the craftsmen of this district put into the place."

Reina: "Who are the ones who took down the beast in the first place?"

Lanson grumbles, unable to argue back with her.

Reina: "And besides, you hate running the regular shop. You always complain how tedious it is and how you want something different to do."

Lanson: "I don't need you telling me that. You've made your point, woman. Now what else do you want? If that is all, I'm returning to my nap."

I can't help but shake my head and let show a small bit of amusement from their interactions. It's like that of a grandfather and granddaughter picking at each other. As snippy as Lanson may be, he never seems to truly be annoyed. I think Reina is the only one to talk to him like that, and he thoroughly enjoys it.

Reina: "What are you shaking your head for, Jale?"

She exclaims this as we start back out the door, finally heading to the northern gate. It still isn't dusk quite yet, but better early than late.

"You and Lanson are quite close."

Reina: "He's been the closest person to me since my father's death. Apart from Enoch, he is one of the few I would call family."

The northern gate has minimal people around it, save for the guards above it.

Reina: "So, I wonder who this mystery cartographer might be. Callaghan said 'him,' didn't he?"

"Yeah, and a cartographer is someone with pretty decent intellect. I wouldn't be looking for anyone young necessarily."

Reina: "Never know really."

"True. Think we should start asking around?"

A child's voice comes from the side of us. We turn to see a young boy. He stands about chest high to me, looking up toward us.

Child: "Are you Jale, sir? They told me to wait here for you and your party. Are you both all that are coming?"

"Coming where? Are you okay, kid?"

Child: "Oh, sorry for not introducing myself. I am the cartographer."

Reina: "Wait, does that mean—"

"Someone as young as you? It's amazing to develop that sort of skill at your age."

Reina: "Jale, no one among the garrison guard is this young."

"What do you mean? How would he know about us then?"

Child: "I think you misjudge my age based on my appearance."

My confusion deepens as Reina stands in some bit of shock as well.

Child: "It seems your friend understands. I'm Hexillico, or Hex for short, actually thirty-one years old, which makes me—"

Reina: "A highlander."

23.

RUMORS

"CARE TO ELABORATE?" I'm not too familiar with highlanders."

Hexillico: "That isn't surprising. Most people who do know anything about us learn from rumor-filled whispers. Please let me know if you want anything clarified for you. We can talk more once we have set out."

The wagon we used to rescue Halister and his people is stocked with a few crates in the front left corner, a large barrel opposite them. Between them is a cutaway to the driver's seat. Lining the sides to the back are bench seats with a small square tile on the floor between them. I'm not sure what it is there for. Three horses idle in front of the cart.

"Do we really need the three? Couldn't the cart be pulled by two?"

Reina: "Sure it can, but the more we have, the faster we could be. Plus, if we need to separate, one could take the extra horse and split off, if need be."

"Guess that makes sense. So, who all is riding along. Is it just us three?"

Reina: "It seems so. I can drive if you want."

Hexillico: "I would rather be in the back, if that is alright. Easier for me to guide us with the map if I have a table to use."

"Table?"

Hexillico goes over to the tile on the floor, lifting it up as the legs fold out from underneath it.

"Fair enough. I guess I will take shotgun."

Reina: "Shotgun?"

"Oh sorry. It means beside the driver."

Reina climbs up the side of the wagon, and I follow suit on the opposite side.

"Hex, you ready back there?"

Hexillico: "All set to head out. Just keep the horses following this way for a while. When the terrain changes, we should head east from then on."

Reina nods and snaps the reins as we set out.

Reina: "So what exactly needs to be clarified about the highlanders, Hex?"

Hexillico: "Well, tell me what your understanding of our people is, and I'd be happy to correct where necessary."

Reina: "Well, the highlanders are known for their reclusive nature up in the mountain ranges."

Hexillico: "Yes, that much is true."

Reina: "Highlanders all retain powerful divinations and are well versed in training others."

Hexillico: "Actually, that part isn't true, though I understand how that falsehood could be taken as truth."

"What makes it false?"

Hexillico: "I'm sure every last one of the highlanders in the badlands is extremely talented with divinations. Sorry, I'm not trying to put myself on a pedestal."

"Wait, so if that is true, why did you say it wasn't?"

Hexillico: "Well, the only reason the highlanders are known for their abilities is because they have to have that level of skill in order to descend from the mountains at all. Those who are weaker would never make it down in the first place."

Reina: "So it's because only the strong make it to the badlands that people assume they are all strong."

"Makes sense. They are the only ones people would ever meet. Hey Hex, what about teaching divinations, is that part true?"

Hex pops his head through the cutout, peeking over the bench Reina and I are sitting on.

Hexillico: "Personally, I've only taught one other person before. I don't know how much more helpful I can be."

"Well, did they learn from your teachings?"

Hexillico: "Yes, but it wasn't like teaching a normal divination."

Reina: "How so?"

Hexillico: "They wanted me to teach them a second divination. This one involved a compass allowing them to trace movements of targets."

Reina: "Wait, you're the one who taught Enoch his dual imbuement technique?!"

Hexillico: "No, no, I only taught him the divination for the compass and assisted him to that end. He came up with the dual imbuement strategy on his own. I wondered for a long while why it was difficult for him to master such a simple divination technique. As it turned out, he only told me after he had successfully activated them at the same time. It stunned me to hear him say so, for that whole time I was so worried I was failing as a teacher if I couldn't even teach one to imbue a small object of a compass. Looking back, I was more relieved to hear it than anything."

"Wow, Enoch is really something for being able to pull it off, it sounds. Is there any among the highlanders who could do the same?"

Hexillico: "I don't think you get how truly amazing it is for Enoch to achieve what he has. It isn't just difficult, it's damn near impossible. His mind must have been put through hell and back. You've gone through the last step in the divination process, right, Jale?"

"Yeah, though it didn't yield anything."

Hexillico: "Now imagine doubling the stress and pain you endured for that."

"Yeah, not something I'd want to do, and on top of all that, I still wasn't able to gain the true divination."

Hexillico: "Exactly. To put imbuement in a simple way, you are pouring your very own consciousness into an object to bend it to your will. That's a feat within itself, and making it stronger, like tempering a blade, is even more so. But to do it like Enoch has, you'd have to split your very consciousness in two."

"How the hell did he manage that?! Wouldn't that drive someone insane, like having dual personalities?"

Hexillico: "I have no idea the effects it'd have. Only Enoch could possibly know the repercussions of activating it. If you heed my warning, you will never attempt to do something like that, else you run a high risk of not just death but becoming one of the Unsettled."

"I don't plan to."

Hexillico: "While we are on the topic, what about you, Jale?"

"What about me?"

Hexillico: "There are certainly rumors and speculation of high-landers, but the same could be said for the Bloodless like yourself."

"Ask away, I guess. Not sure what I can tell you, though. I haven't met another like myself yet."

Hexillico: "It's said that Bloodless have an incredible amount of physical strength unmatched by their past physical forms."

"Yeah, that's definitely true. I don't recall being weak in my past, but I have underestimated the amount of force I retain in this form."

Hexillico: "Astonishing. The other rumors revolve around Bloodless being mindless beings without the ability to speak, but that clearly isn't true."

"Well, like I said, I have no idea about others like me. It could be that I am an outlier."

The terrain darkens from the bright orange sands to a dark brown dirt. Actual soil—something I have yet to see in this place.

"Woah, is this the terrain change you meant, Hex?"

Hexillico: "Yep, you can go a bit farther inland to get away from the sands, but then start heading east."

Reina: "Gotcha."

Hexillico: "Jale, you were also the first one to refute the rumors surrounding Solomon and his army. Seems as though you have a knack for discerning information. The commandant told me all about you in the meeting."

"Yeah, he didn't seem to be my biggest fan at the time."

Hexillico: "Ha, ha. don't go assuming. Isn't that what created the very rumors we aim to dismiss?"

"Right, what did he say?"

Hexillico: "Even if you were in disagreement with one another for a bit, he respects you for taking a stance, even if it is against the grain."

"What's the story between him and Garrett? They didn't seem to get along at all. Is it the same kind of respect they share?"

Hexillico: "You wouldn't believe me if I said those two are closer than anyone else in the district. They love to pester each other and argue, but it strengthens their bond. Those who would be adversaries couldn't remain civil with each other like those two can."

"Yeah, I think you're right."

Hexillico: "About?"

"About not believing you."

Hex laughs as he goes back to sitting down at his table in the back, pulling out his map and fixing it down to the table with clamps. Reina steers the horses east after we can no longer see the sands that were once behind us.

We ride for a while under the crescent moon, as the sun set not long into our journey. A light breeze embraces us as I lean back on the wagon's seat. It amuses me, the drastic changes in temperature that can occur in the day-to-night cycle of badlands. Wheels gently rock against the dry dirt, enough to lull me to sleep. To keep myself awake, I question Hex further.

"Hey, Hex?"

Hexillico: "Yes? Something wrong?"

"No, just wondering, how much of the badlands have you marked on that map of yours?"

Hexillico: "A decent amount. I can get around from district to district, but there are several places I couldn't journey to alone, hence the cover for this mission given to me by the commandant."

"Oh yeah, that is the reason on paper. Ah, and one more thing: What is that district called?"

Hexillico: "What is it called? What do you mean?"

"Exactly what I said. What's the name of the district. It does have a name, doesn't it?"

Reina: "Wow . . . that's a good point. We haven't really had the need to travel to other districts, so I guess we never differentiated between them."

Hexillico: "I guess none of the districts really have names."

"With this ongoing feud, I imagine we may have to travel to many districts. Here's a thought: As the cartographer, why don't you give them names yourself? I'm sure labeling them would give those who utilize these maps a better understanding of where they may be."

Hexillico: "Good point, but how about this: Since you came up with the idea, you be the first one to name one. What should our own district be named from this point on?"

"Pushing it back on me, huh? You'll have to give me a second to—"

The ground beneath us starts to shake as the gentle sway of the wheels becomes more like a jostle. I hold onto my seat as Reina whips the reins and pulls the wagon aside.

"What the hell?"

Hexillico: "Found us faster than I anticipated. Jale, Reina, get ready!"

24.
AMNESTY

I JUMP OFF THE WAGON, rifle in my hands, peering across the desolate lands. A weirdly strong sweet smell starts to fill the air around us. The horses stamp their hooves on the ground in a panic.

"What found us? I'm not seeing anything, Hex!"

Reina on the other side calls back to us as well.

Reina: "Nothing on this side either!"

Hexillico: "We aren't going to be able to see it till it's too late."

Hex jumps down from the back of the wagon and unfolds a scythe-like object from it.

Hexillico: "Reina, this side please!"

Reina jumps up to the wagon then down beside us both. Hex slams the handle of the scythe into the ground as the blade cuts in a circle around the center.

"What are you doing?"

Hexillico: "My divination. Please allow me to concentrate."

Eight lines in the dirt form without ever having the scythe blade cut into it. The cardinal and ordinal directions mark themselves as the blade begins to circle around, stopping as it points in the southeast.

Hexillico: "It's coming from that way. Get ready!"

The dirt mounds not more than ten feet from us as a creature with the face of a human being pops up from the soil, as does a pair of arms, yet the rest of its body writhes like a worm as it leaps toward us. Hex turns the blade toward it and pushes the handle of the scythe up in a crescent-shaped motion, piercing straight through the creature's torso. Lifelessly, it falls to the ground. Hex places his foot on it and pulls out the scythe.

"What is that thing?"

Reina stands in shock as she props her hand up, leaning against the wagon and breathing heavily.

Hexillico: "One of the many reasons why Greed and his forces don't give chase to Wrath. Out here, lying in wait, are Unsettled that choose to ambush their prey with only moments of warning."

Hex turns back as he folds up his scythe-like weapon and pushes it under the table where his map lies atop. Reina regains her composure, joining us at the rear of the wagon.

Reina: "Well, that was eventful. Definitely not something you should warn us of beforehand."

Hexillico: "I was instructed not to as a means of preventing the two of you from changing your minds. I apologize for it, but I was confident in my ability to handle these creatures since I am one of the few who have braved these lands prior."

"So, what are they?"

Hexillico: "This type of Unsettled is known as a Banshee. Like I said before, they are an ambush predator."

Reina: "How do you intend to proceed? We can't exactly expect to track down Wrath while simultaneously fending off constant ambushes."

Hex points over at the dead carcass.

Hexillico: "This ambush wasn't unexpected in the first place, and our solution lies closer than you think. That scent you are picking up—it's from these Banshees."

Reina: "How will that help us?"

Hexillico: "Banshees don't hunt in packs like wolves or coyotes. Having multiple in a single area scares off prey due to the heavier vibrations felt in the ground."

Hex heads over to the Banshee, cutting off the tip of its tail and making a hole in it as he pushes a rope through and ties it off. The sweet smell from the tail becomes more intense as he nails it to the side of the wagon.

Hexillico: "Banshees have an incredible sense of smell. Though they lack good eyesight and are sensitive to light, they can still track prey by both smell and vibration. Normally they have to use smell, because vibrations alone can't identify prey."

Reina: "You think this is how Wrath moves his people across the badlands as well?"

Hexillico: "Most likely. I learned this trick a while back whilst scouting this area for the first time, though I knew nothing then of the Banshees when I descended from my home in the mountains. A trader's caravan I had been riding with told me of them and even sold me a necklace made from one of their corpses. I had no reason not to believe them, and even if it were a lie, it only cost me five copper. Better safe than sorry I guess."

Reina: "What happened to the necklace?"

Hexillico: "It stopped giving off the sweet smell that warded off these beasts. I think I still have it somewhere in my room back in the district. The point is, the smell doesn't last forever, so we best make haste now. We could take on another of this size relatively easily, but the larger they become, the more difficult they'll be to deal with."

"Just seems to be getting crazier and crazier every day, doesn't it?"

Hexillico: "Just a sign we are making headway."

Reina: "That's an optimistic way to look at it."

We pile back into the wagon. This time I take the reins and let Reina rest for a bit in the back. Hex joins me, riding shotgun as I calm the horses and we begin to move out.

Hexillico: "I don't relish keeping secrets you know."

"Why do you bring that up?"

Hexillico: "Because of the danger I could have put the both of you in. I was confident I could handle it, but I'd be lying if I said I had no doubts at all."

"Reina was quite a bit shook up, but I don't think she'd hold it against you."

I look back, and Reina is passed out on one of the benches. She had been up quite a bit earlier than me, preparing for this journey.

"They were orders from a superior as well, and besides, you took good care of us, dispatching that thing as swiftly as it had appeared."

Hexillico: "Thanks, Jale, but . . ."

"Something else you want to get off your chest?"

Hexillico: "Yeah, the Banshees . . . they weren't the only thing I was to keep from you."

"What else was there, then?"

Hexillico: "Another assignment for this mission was to monitor your progress in divination."

"Is that all?"

Hexillico: "If at any time you seemed to be turning into one of those things, I was to . . . end your life beforehand."

A long moment of silence proceeds as I think about it.

Hexillico: "I'm sorry, Jale, I hope you can forgive me."

"Forgive? I like that."

Hexillico: "Huh?"

"Amnesty. That is what we will call our own district. To be pardoned from this world, a place where we can begin to fight for a better tomorrow. What do you think?"

Hexillico: "A bit off topic, but I do like it. You aren't mad?"

"No, I'm actually quite pleased, Hex, do what you have to. If my life came to an end to save those around me, well, that would please me. Knowing I had not held any of you back. If that does happen, give me everything you got. I'd rather fall to the hands of a person like you while I'm still myself, rather than cause others grief. I have done enough of that for one lifetime."

Hex looks away, his hands folded in his lap.

Hexillico: "Well, I don't want to have to do it at all."

"You may—"

Hexillico: No! I won't have to, because under my guidance . . ."

He looks back to me, eyes dried from tears.

Hexillico: "Under my guidance, you will master your divination. I won't allow you to force me to make a cruel decision like that, understand?"

I pat him on his shoulder. Such a strong will like his—I'm glad I got to meet him.

"With pleasure. Now let's go track down the Grand Sin of Wrath."

FIN

JALE

ENOCH

FAYNE

HALISTER

HEXILLICO

REINA

SOLOMON

BOOK 2 TEASER

"I WON'T MAKE THIS AN EASY FIGHT."

It's been a week and a half on Wrath's trail. The sun hasn't bothered us near as much as I thought it would. Hex has used the spare time we share to improve my divination. To start, he wanted me to figure out how to attack with it. I struggled for a while, but looking back on it, the answer was much simpler than I had made it out to be.

When I first was given my dowsing rods, they arrived on a stone pillar that had shifted up from the sands. A stone pillar! The tool for my attack was right there in front of me this whole time. That being said, my first attempt was still pitiful at best. Reina let out a hearty laugh when no more than an ant mound popped up from my efforts. Hex encouraged me through it, though. Now it's not quite the pillar from before but something resembling a stalagmite, which I can produce all in a single moment, sprouting like a flower from the sands. The largest I've been able to conjure was almost four feet tall. Next, we moved on to my creating multiple pillars at once. It was mentally exhausting, but I managed the bare minimum—the word *multiple* being the important thing at that point. They weren't tall, two and a half feet at best, but they were enough to knock someone flat, if placed properly. And if there is something I am good at, I would have to say it's placement. Maybe it's from what Galahad taught me about control, but I can make those stalagmites rise from the ground nearly anywhere in eyesight.

After the first week, we sparred easily a dozen times. The first time, I wasn't even able to touch Hex. The way he avoids every placement I conjure is inhuman. Perhaps it's another amazing highlander skill to add to the long list. Must be from his directional divination—he can sense where I'm attacking almost as fast as I activate it. Not to mention, he has yet to even pick up his scythe after his initial casting. If he uses his scythe, I won't last a minute.

Hex is a good teacher, though. Damn good. My progress has been remarkable, even to me. Before, I couldn't even imagine doing what I am today, but here we are. Still, when he takes his stance to spar, he becomes quite smug. Makes me want to land at least one clean hit on him. Thus far I have managed to throw him off balance a few times and nicked his shin once, but nothing substantial. His directional divination can even redirect mine back at me. Learned that the hard way when I engaged him in close quarters and casted it toward him. I got a stone straight to the gut for that slipup. Hex is a crafty one, and I can't see myself winning by any means. But that doesn't mean I'll go down easy. If he thinks that, he's got another thing coming.

Hex: "Come on, Jale, this is our fifth match of the day. I know you want to learn quickly, but getting your ass handed to you won't help you learn, you know?"

ACKNOWLEDGMENTS

ARTISTS

The experience of seeing something you've painstakingly created come to life, from just simple words on a page that only I as the author could visualize, to vibrant scenes that could be shared the world over, is something wondrous. Throughout every chapter I commissioned, I never once tired of the excitement that each new image brought. To see my world made real, from my imagination to art, inspired me to keep going no matter how long the wait. It's not an understatement to say that my book wouldn't be complete without the help of these two amazing artists.

@Fera__Blue (X)

@_xenefia (X)

CONCEPT ARTISTS

All the art within started with the character design. Before a single scene, background, or even any color at all, it was a few rough sketches from a variety of artists that brought my story to where it is now. These pieces, though seemingly small, laid the foundation that the finished art was buit upon. This led, in turn, to finding my main artists, who refined those concepts into the final renditions seen today. So, with great pleasure, I thank them for their contributions here.

@alin_laphel (X)

@CRUVOD (X)

@Vulpus16 (X)

Kmmdy_.9070 (Discord)

nizma03 (Discord)

zhakiro (Discord)

NARRATIVE HELP

Refinement comes with time and perseverance. Initially I underestimated just how trying this stage would be. Writing a story, that's not the hard part; it's honing out its imperfections. Scrutinizing each and every word, the phrasing, making certain not to repeat oneself. It was stressful to say the least. With the help of both my editor and publisher, it is now at the finest point possible from a narrative perspective. Thank you for all the help.

Emily Hitchcock (Publisher)

Clair Fink (Publisher)

Sarah Herchenroether (Developmental Editor)

Jennifer Pellman (Copy Editor)

Heather Shaw (Proofreader)

ACKNOWLEDGMENTS

FIGHT CHOREOGRAPHY

Sweat the small stuff. No, literally—sweat it. One of the coolest things to do is to depict the realism of a world made to be fantasy. Blend the fantastical with the factual. To this end I put my physical self in the place of Jale. In each scenario, my instructor taught me not only how to write it but how to perform the movements myself. Be it disarming an opponent, knocking them off balance, or taking them down to the ground. My friend and trainer put his expertise to good use, quite literally throwing me into the fold.

Alex Earwood (Martial Arts Trainer)

TEST READERS

"Bone-rattlingly interesting, I can't wait for more!"

"Definitely an amazing book, an immersive story with an adventure twist."

As an author, nothing means more than to see the positive reactions of the first fans of what's planned to be an adventurous series. A single word of encouragement to say I'm going in the right direction can be enough to push past the droughts of inspiration. Thank you to those who kept me going.

chaselocalyanderefan (Discord)

Primordialgrilledchez (Discord)

Kindra Dobbins

FRIENDS AND FAMILY

Whether bouncing ideas back and forth, or just lending an ear to hear me ramble, my family and friends have been with me from the very start. In person or online, it doesn't seem like much, but it gave me the push in the right direction each and every time. Before I knew it, my book had spurred a small community on my own personal Discord server as well as on X. I know it's more generic to say, but I appreciate everyone who stood behind me along the way.

Rocky Carroll

Trevor Carroll

Tim Dobbins

Haylee Dobbins

Michael Dunn

Teresa Dunn

Robert Dunn

Travis (Will) Downs

Jesse Mckee

Harrison Brown

Angel Quiles

And many others. The truth is, if I had to list out everyone, I don't think I would publish for a long time to come. So, in short, thank you to the wonderful and ever-expanding community of family and friends encouraging me at every step!

ABOUT THE AUTHOR

MARSHALL CARROLL grew up in the rural area of Newark, Ohio. He spent his childhood involved in multiple extracurricular activities including football, wrestling, baseball, and competitive dance in hip-hop and jazz at Patty's Dance Center. Marshall studied advanced classes in high school, heavily favoring history at Licking Valley High School. Marshall developed an interest in guns and airsoft and formed his own airsoft club along with his friends who shared his interest. What had started as just a Saturday hobby, with only him and his close friends, grew to multiple participants from many locations. Eventually, there were so many participants, they were divided into two separate teams comprised of NATO and Rusfor. Marshall now participates in mass airsoft events with over a thousand participants across the United States. In addition to airsoft, Marshall has trained in several styles and forms of martial arts, including Brazilian Jui Jitsu, kickboxing, Muay Thai, Judo, Krav Maga, and even Iaido at Impact Family Martial Arts. This training is directly reflected in his writing, makng the fight scenes have more realism and depth. Outside of extracurricular activities, Marshall is an avid gamer and anime fan. Some inspirations for his writing include his favorites games, *Fallout New Vegas* and *Metal Gear Solid*. Anime inspirations include *Jobless Reincarnation*, *Gate*, and *Hunter x Hunter*. Marshall has always been an animal lover, with a special affinity for cats. His current cats that comfort him in between his page writing and activities are Comet, Sage, Benny, Bonnie, and Clyde. Marshall is a middle child of three, with an older brother and younger sister. In the future, Marshall strives to improve his physique via cardio and weightlifting to assist his martial arts and airsoft activities. In addition, he seeks to expand this single novel into a series with a supportive community fanbase that eagerly awaits each release.

www.ingramcontent.com/pod-product-compliance
Lightning Source LLC
Chambersburg PA
CBHW050129030726
47505CB00007B/2102